Brander Matthews

The Story of a Story, and Other Stories

Brander Matthews

The Story of a Story, and Other Stories

ISBN/EAN: 9783743399778

Manufactured in Europe, USA, Canada, Australia, Japa

Cover: Foto ©Andreas Hilbeck / pixelio.de

Manufactured and distributed by brebook publishing software (www.brebook.com)

Brander Matthews

The Story of a Story, and Other Stories

THE STORY OF A STORY

AND OTHER STORIES

BY

BRANDER MATTHEWS

ILLUSTRATED

NEW YORK

HARPER & BROTHERS PUBLISHERS

1893

I take pleasure in inscribing these stories to

T. B. ALDRICH

From whom I learnt the trade
of story-telling.

CONTENTS

THE NEW MEMBER OF THE CLUB.

ETELKA TALMEYR: A Tale of Three Cities.

ILLUSTRATIONS

THE STORY OF A STORY

THE STORY OF A STORY

I.—THE AUTHOR.

THE author turned on his couch uneasily
as he was dictating the final paragraphs of
his story.   His wife sat writing at a table
by the window.   In the little square far
down below them there were signs of spring;
the first touch of warmer weather had been
felt, and the trees were beginning to bud
out timidly.   The afternoon sun fell aslant
the floor in long lines of feeble light.   The
invalid looked out towards the west and
caught a glimpse of the floating clouds red-
dening as the day waned.   He gazed at them
as though anxious to borrow their golden
hues to color his words.

His wife finished setting on paper the last
sentence he had dictated.   She waited si-

lently for the next, but in a moment she looked up.

"What is it, dear?" she asked, when she saw the look on his face.

"We shall have another glorious sunset to-day," he answered. "How lucky it is that we live so high up in the air that we can see them."

"Shall I raise you up?" she inquired, hastily.

"Not yet," he responded; "I must finish the story first. Where was I?"

She took up the sheets of manuscript which lay before her and replied, "I had just written this: 'In morals, as in geometry, the straight line is the shortest distance between two points; and John Strang never swerved from the swift path. He was alone, but a true hero needs no other witness than his own conscience—'"

"I know, I know," the author interrupted; "a couple of hundred words more and the work is done. I'm going to wind it up short and sharp, and give the reader a real surprise. 'He strode forward fearlessly. Out of the darkness there came to meet him—'"

Having begun again to dictate, the sick
man with an obvious effort braced himself
as he lay, and continued until he reached
the end of the tale, pausing but for an instant now and again to find the fit word, at
once simple and strong, to carry his meaning. The last few sentences fell from his
lips swiftly, tumbling one over another in
the haste of their maker to be at the goal of
his desires; and his amanuensis had to let
her pen speed over the paper to keep pace
with her husband's rapid speech. At last
the story-teller concluded, "'So it came to
pass that John Strang conquered himself,
and thus he was spared the knowledge that
the saddest of all joys is a satisfied vengeance.'" The tension of his task relaxed
all at once, the author fell back on his pil-
low, and the westering sun cast a rosy light
on his pale, thin face, with its eager eyes
and its determined mouth. He watched his
wife while she wrote this final sentence, and
then he said, "That is all."

She numbered the page she had just com-
pleted, and laid it on top of the others.

His eyes followed her movements wistfully, and then he looked anxiously into her face, as though waiting for her judgment on his labor.

When he found that she was intent on sorting the pages in order and did not speak, he broke the silence himself.

"I'm afraid it is not very good?" he said, tentatively.

She looked up and smiled at him proudly. "It is one of the best things you have ever done," she declared.

The color on his cheeks deepened a little —but perhaps the sun was responsible for this—and the light came back to his eye.

"I'm afraid that it is not very new," he returned, doubtfully.

"It is the old, old story," she rejoined, firmly, "and that is always new and always true; and it always will be as long as there is an honest man and woman in the world."

"The whole thing is so fresh to me now," he said, with a hint of rising confidence in his weary voice, "that I don't know anything at all about it. By to-morrow I shall be ready to call it poor stuff, I suppose. If it is good for anything, I shall not find it out until I get the proof from the magazine."

"Where are you going to send it?" asked his wife.

"To *The Metropolis*, I think," he responded. "They read there more promptly than anywhere else, and they pay better, too."

"They didn't give you much for that last story of yours they took," she rejoined.

"Well, they didn't like that story very much, and perhaps they were right," he said. "After it had been out a month or so I went in and looked over the scrap-book of newspaper notices, and hardly one of them said a word about my story."

"What does a newspaper man know about literature?" asked the author's wife, indignantly.

"You know that they spoke to me about writing a serial for them; that shows that they like my work," said the author, "and perhaps this story will please them better. I think the fight ought to be popular; I tried to make it a good fight—"

"And you did," she interrupted; "I

got so excited over it I could hardly write."

"I wished to have it a good fight in it. self," he continued, "and at the same time typical of the eternal strife of good and evil. Yet I don't know whether I really want any- body to suspect the allegory or not. I think I like stories best when the moral is quite concealed."

"You haven't flaunted your moral in the reader's face, if that's what you mean," she returned. "But it's there all the same; and I don't doubt it 'll do good too. I like the man; he's a gentleman and a man at the same time. And I could fall in love with the heroine; she's lovely, and noble, and womanly, and feminine, too!"

He looked her full in the face, and there was a touching sweetness in his voice as he said, "How can I ever draw any other kind of woman—when I have so fine a model be- fore me?"

She rose from the little table by the win- dow and crossed over to his couch. He held out his hand—a long, delicately modelled hand—and she clasped it.   Then she bent over and kissed him.

The author smiled up at her again, though a sudden twist of pain stiffened the lines of his face, and beads of chill perspiration began to form on his brow.   She knew the signs of coming suffering, and her heart sank; but she still smiled at him with her mouth and her eyes as she moved away to prepare the medicine it was now time for him to take.

II.—THE EDITOR.

The ample offices of *The Metropolis*, an illustrated monthly magazine, filled a floor of a broad building in Broadway.   The publisher, with his assistants and with half a score of book-keepers and clerks, occupied the front of the loft, and the editorial rooms and the art department were crowded together in the rear of the building.   The private office of the editor-in-chief was to be reached only by passing through the rooms in which sat his associates, and he was thus in a measure protected from the intrusion of the bores and the cranks.

One Monday morning towards the latter part of May, two or three weeks after the author had made an end of dictating the story to his wife as he lay on his customary couch of pain, the editor sat in this inner office in consultation with his principal assistant.

"Have you got the schedule for the midsummer number there?" asked the editor.

His assistant, whose duty it was to "make up" the magazine, handed the editor a sheet of paper strangely ruled and half covered with penciled notes.

"I want to see if we can't make room for this story," said the editor, taking a folded manuscript from the little hand-bag he always carried to and from his own house, where he absented himself often that he might read the more important contributions at leisure.

"How long is it?" asked the assistant.

"Between eight and nine thousand words," the editor answered. "It is a breezy, out-door thing, well suited to a sum-

mer number, and there's a fight in it that
will be a relief to the quietness of the serial.
In fact, this story will help to balance the
midsummer fiction in a way I like."

"Well," responded the subordinate, "we
can get it in, if you insist, although it will be
a tight squeeze to pack in nine thousand
words. Must it be illustrated? That'll
make it all the harder."

"One picture will be enough, at any rate,"
the editor rejoined.

"Then I think I see how to work it," said
the assistant, after consulting the schedule.
"We'll put the picture at the end of the
second cut form and run in a plain form
next. That ought to do it nicely; and of
course we can tuck in a poem to fill up the
last page if we have to."

"All right," assented the editor.

The assistant added a few suggestions,
words, and figures to the schedule; and
then he looked up and remarked: "The
artist will have to hump himself if we are
going to get the plate in time for the midsummer. That comes out the last week in
July, and here we are near the end of May.

All the other cuts are done; at least they told me yesterday they expected the last one in to-day."

"There's that new man just back from Paris," said the editor, "that pupil of Gérôme's they have been talking about in the art department. They might let him do it."

"I don't believe that the public really likes those impressionist scratches," the assistant responded; "but they say this man is a quick worker, and he is anxious for a job. I suppose we can risk it."

"Then you had better talk to them about it this morning," the editor declared, "and see that he gets the manuscript at once."

The assistant took the flat package of folded paper and began to discuss another subject: "Don't you think we ought to have a taking title for that yarn about yachting in the Pacific? How would 'From China to Peru' do?"

III.—THE ARTIST.

There is a little restaurant in a little house on a little street not far from a cluster of studio-buildings, and one of the many young artists who frequent it intermittently once called it "The Fried Cat," and by that picturesque but doubtful name the little restaurant has ever since been known.

The specialty of "The Fried Cat" was a fifty-cent dinner, wine and coffee included. This was served in three little rooms, opening one into the other and containing perhaps a score of small square tables.

On a rainy evening in the last week of May a dozen or so of these tables were occupied. At one of them, near the open French windows that looked into the little yard behind the restaurant, sat three young men smoking their cigarettes with their coffee. The tallest of them was the artist who had recently returned from Paris, where he had studied at the Beaux Arts under M. Gérôme.

"I hear you are working for *The Metropolis*," said one of his friends, a young poet who supported himself by editing a society weekly.

"They've been after me to do something for them ever since I got back," responded the artist, rolling a fresh cigarette and lighting it with the stump of the old one. "I don't care much to do black-and-white. Color is my stronghold, you know, though I'm not afraid of line. But I wanted to collar the dollars, and, besides, it's good practice."

"What is the story like?" asked the poet.

"The story?" echoed the artist. "Oh, the story isn't much. At least I don't care for that kind of stuff—heroism, you know— Romeo and Juliet, and all that sort of thing. But there's a fight in it, a fight on a lot of sand-dunes, and I've done them a regular Cazin. It isn't easy to get real *plein-airiste* effects into a black-and-white, but I think I've got 'em this time."

"Is it done already?" inquired the third man at the table, a sad-looking young fellow who wrote comic sketches for the weekly papers.

"Oh yes," answered the artist. "I glanced over the story last night, and this morning I got me a model, and I knocked off the sketch in two or three hours."

"Oils or pen-and-ink?" the poet queried.

"Oh, oils, of course," the artist responded; "and they are going to process it like those 'Tartarin' things, you know."

"How will it come out?" the humorist asked.

"Oh, I don't know," said the artist, "and I don't much care. I'm to have my sketch back, and if the cut isn't good I can make a water-color of the subject for one of the fall exhibitions. I believe I could make a lovely water-cooler of it—*tout pourri de chic*, you know."

IV.—THE PRINTER.

Early in June there came a spell of intensely hot weather such as often lends unexpectedness to the New York spring. Nowhere were the effects of the heat more unpleasant than in the long, low rooms where worked the compositors employed by the company that printed *The Metropolis*. Pending the completion of a spacious building in the course of construction next door, the whole force of the large printing establishment was crowded into three adjoining private houses hastily and incommodiously altered to serve as a makeshift while the new edifice was going up. Even at midday in June, when the longest day in the year was close at hand, the light was insufficient; and the men who stood in their shirtsleeves at the tall cases near the middle of the narrow room had to rely for illumination on flaring gas-jets that added to the heat of the loft and to the foulness of the air.

When the shrill whistle announced the end of the noon hour of rest, a huge, blond German printer took his place beneath one of these gas-jets and grumbled as he gazed down at the sheets of manuscript he had taken from the copy-hook. These were pages of the story the author had dictated to his wife.

" Was fur schreiben sind diese ?" he growl-

ed, as he examined the fine and delicate cal-
ligraphy of the lady. "Himmel! vy don'd
dese Amerigan women write like Ghris-
tians? Vas dere effer such scrieben. als
diese? Ugh! Und I come in late, dinkin'
I might ged a fat take on dat cyglobedia!
Vell, I must vollow gopy, I suppose; it is
bud four or five schdigs I have."

Still grumbling, he hung the sheets of
manuscript on a hook at the head of his
case and took up his composing-stick. As
he was adjusting his broad spectacles over
his solid nose to see what he was to set up,
the gas-jet over his head flared up and then
went out suddenly.

"Ach, himmel!" cried the printer in dis-
gust, as he tried to set the gas-fixture in order. "Das arbeitet nicht. Muss mann es
fixiren!"

V.—THE PUBLISHER.

On the last day of June a full set of
sheets of the midsummer number of *The
Metropolis* were laid on the desk of the
publisher of that magazine; and he spent

2

an hour or more in examining them carefully and in deciding upon the best means
of calling to them the attention of the
public.

Three or four times the publisher came
back to the story which the author had dictated and which the artist had illustrated.
At last he touched a bell and told the boy
who came in response to this summons to
go to the assistant editor and to request
that the assistant editor would please be so
kind as to come in to see the publisher on
his way out to lunch.

Towards one o'clock, when the assistant
editor came in, the publisher asked, " When
do you send out your literary notes about
the midsummer number ?"

" Between the 15th and 20th, I suppose,"
answered the assistant editor.   " There are
lots of good things in the midsummer to
hang a note on."

" If it's just the same to you," the publisher continued, " I wish you wouldn't send
out a note about the story this picture illus-
trates," and he pointed to a full-page drawing wherein two men were engaged in dead-

ly combat on a strip of sand running out into the sea.

" We don't often make any preliminary announcement of mere short stories, you know," the assistant editor explained.

" Then that's all right," said the publish-er. " You see I don't want to seem to bear down too hard on any one thing. Now I like this picture. It will make a first-rate poster."

" That's so," assented the assistant editor, seeing at once the effectiveness of the scene for the purpose of arresting the vagrant at-tention of the casual magazine-buyer at a news-stand or in a book-store.

" And if I use the picture on all our post-ers," the publisher explained, " it seems to me better to say nothing about the story in the advance notes."

VI.—THE CRITIC.

The night before the midsummer number of the magazine was published, copies were sent out to the daily newspapers for review. In the office of the *Gotham Gazette* the mag-   •

azines of the month were regarded not as literature but as news. They were not criticised by one of the literary critics of the journal, but by one of the minor editorial writers of the paper, who was wont to run rapidly over the pages of every review and monthly magazine as it arrived, submitting to the managing editor any article which seemed likely to furnish a text for a column of brevier, and penning a hasty paragraph or two in which he recorded the impressions of his cursory perusal.

Thus it was that on the morning of August 1st the *Gotham Gazette* printed upon its editorial page in solid minion these words :

" The midsummer number of *The Metropolis* is neither better nor worse than the conductors of this admirably illustrated magazine have accustomed us to. The frontispiece is a portrait of William Dunlap, who helped to found the National Academy of Design, and who wrote a history of the theatre in America ; the face of the picture is interesting but rather weak ; and the accompanying article is weak and not interesting. 'From China to Peru' is the illustrated record of a daring voyage in a ten-ton sloop, almost as good as one of Mr. Robert White's delightful marines. An anonymous writer discusses 'The Natural History of Games,' and shows how modern scientific theories account for the survival of the sports best fitted for a given people at a given time; thus the game of poker, for example, seemingly invented by brave fellows of Queen Elizabeth's day (when it was known as primero), was revived in the very nick of time to serve the needs of the Argonauts of Forty-nine. The 'Hills of the Sky' is a pleasantly written and amply illustrated account of the colony of authors and artists at Onteora in the Catskills. Under the modest and somewhat misleading title of 'The Strange Misadventures of a Blue Pencil' a member of the staff of the *Gotham Gazette* contributes a fresh and picturesque description of the making of a great daily newspaper. In 'Pasticcio'—the new department for humorous odds and ends—there is a rather pretentious screed, 'On the Wise Choice of a Mother-in-Law,' which some readers will doubtless consider funny.

"Mr. Rupert de Ruyter continues his serial, 'The Poor Islanders,' which is now
seen to be a rather bitter attack on British
'society;' Mr. de Ruyter is best known as a
poet, but this novel shows that he is a master of prose as well. The rest of the fiction
in this number of *The Metropolis* does not
call for comment; perhaps the best of the
three short stories is a rather high-flown,
semi-realistic tale of young love triumphant,
an old enough story, but yet told with a certain freshness."

VII.—TWO YOUNG READERS.

On the first Saturday evening in August
there was a gathering of young people in a
house built on a rock and projecting its
deep piazzas over the waters of Narragan-
sett Bay within sight of Point Judith. The
owner of the place had sons and daughters,
and these sons and daughters had each a
friend; and so it was that there was a house-
ful of company, and that the easy laughter
of young men and maidens filled the broad

hall and the wide parlors.   There had been
lawn-tennis all the afternoon on the smooth
sward which sloped gently away on one side
of the house, with its grass almost as green-
ly beautiful as the close-cropped turf of England; then there had been a late dinner en-
livened by the humor of a young lawyer, a
comrade of the eldest son, and able to leave
the city only from Friday to Monday; and
now there was a little music in one of the
parlors, where a group was gathered about
a piano singing the old war-songs and the
older college - songs, and changing from
" Marching through Georgia " to " Lauriger
Horatius."

The young lawyer from New York had
strolled out on the piazza with the eldest
daughter of the house, his junior by two or
three years.   The young people walked to
and fro before the open window of the parlor where the others were making merry.
He was a handsome young fellow, with
hopeful eyes and a resolute mouth.   She
was a good-looking girl, thoughtful and yet
lively.

As they walked they talked of trifles—of

the weather, of the tennis that afternoon, of the city election the next fall, of the moonlight which silvered the waves that washed the rocks below them.

" There is the night boat," he said, pointing to a dark shape in the distance sparkling with electric lights and speeding swiftly over the water towards Point Judith.

" Isn't this like a scene in the theatre ?" she returned. " It is so beautiful that it seems unreal."

" Suppose we go out to the summer-house and take it all in ?" he suggested.

One of the piazzas extended beyond the house to the very verge of the rocks, and here there was a summer-house, with a hammock swung from a pair of its posts.

" Hadn't you better get into the hammock ?" he asked, when they had reached the summer-house. " You have been playing tennis all the afternoon."

" But I'm not a bit tired," she responded, as she settled herself in the net-work and began to swing lazily in the moonlight. " And yet this is restful, I confess."

Just then the group about the piano in

the parlor a few yards behind them changed from " Rally Round the Flag " to " Come where my love lies dreaming."

The moonbeams fell on the clear, pale skin of the girl in the hammock, and the young man thought he had never seen her look so lovely ; and the desire to tell her how much he loved her, and to tell her that very evening, at once, and without dangerous delay, arose within him irresistibly.

" This is really delightful," she said, when the silence had lasted a minute or two, " to swing here in the moonlight on a Saturday night, when the work of the week is done. Don't you like it ?"

" I ?" he responded.   " Don't I !"

" Then take a chair and sit down to enjoy it."

" To hear is to obey," he answered, and he drew forward a camp-stool.   As it came out of the shadow something fell from the seat.   He stooped and picked it up.

· " It's only a magazine," he explained.

" Oh yes," she returned, as a faint flush came into her cheeks.   " It's *The Metropolis*, isn't it ?"

"Yes," he answered, glancing down at the magazine in his hand; "it's the August number."

"I had it out here this morning," she continued, hastily, "to read that story you were speaking about last night."

"The one I had read in the train coming here?" he returned. "I remember now. And how did you like it?"

"It was splendid," she responded, with interest. "There was too much fighting, but it was thrilling, and the hero was a real hero."

"Well, I thought he was more of a real man than most of the heroes we see in books," the young lawyer replied.

"Of course the girl was a goose," the young lady went on.

"Oh!" cried the young man, a little taken aback. "Do you know, I rather liked that girl?"

"Oh no!" persisted the occupant of the hammock, sitting up suddenly. "I'm sure you didn't! I don't see how any man could ever *love* a creature like that. Could you?"

"It is easy to answer that question," said the young man, as his heart gave a bound. "I could love only one woman in the world; I do love only one woman; I can never love any other."

Then he paused for a moment. The color went out of her face, but she said nothing.

"You know who she is," he went on passionately; "you are not blind. You know that I love *you*."

Here he dropped on his knees beside the hammock and seized her hand.

"I love you!" he repeated, fervently. "Can you love me a little?"

She made no answer in words, but there was a clasping of the hand he held. Then he threw his arms about her as she lay in the hammock and kissed her.

The music still went on in the parlor; the moonlight still danced across the waves; the night boat was still visible in the distance; the external world was still what it had been but a minute ago; yet to the young people in the summer-house life had never seemed so fair before.

VIII.—ONE OLD READER.

The next Saturday was a day of intense heat; it was the last and worst of five days of inexorably rising temperature; it was a day when every man who could fled from town as from a fiery furnace. In the afternoon, as the great stores closed, tired shop-girls and salesmen came forth limply rejoicing that their half-day's work was done. In the side streets, where the tall tenement-houses towered aloft, weary mothers strove in vain to soothe their fretful children. The horses of the street-cars staggered along hopelessly, as though they knew that for them there was no surcease of labor. Even when the fleeting twilight began to settle down upon the city there was no relief from the heat.

About seven o'clock that evening a little old maid was riding in a car of a line which twisted about through noisome neighborhoods, ill-kept and foul even in winter, and now wellnigh suffocating. She was a trim little old woman, neatly dressed, well shod, properly gloved. She was obviously well-to-do, and if she lingered in town in the thick of the heated term it was at the call of duty. Ever since a rebel bullet had made her a widow before she was a wife the little old maid had given herself to works of charity; and it was in midsummer, when most of the charitable people are away, that she had the heaviest demands upon her. She took but a scant vacation every year, and it was taken always in Lent.

On that hot and intolerable Saturday evening in August the little old maid was returning from a day of unselfish and unpleasant toil in a tenement-house where she had been serving as a volunteer nurse. She was worn with the work and glad of the restful motion of the car. She held in her hand a magazine—the midsummer number of *The Metropolis;* but the jaded horses had drawn her for nearly half a mile before she opened its pages. Even when she finally took it up she turned the leaves with tired inattention until a chance sentence in a short story caught her eye :

"The future is not rosier to youth than is the past to age."

Then the little old maid turned back to the beginning of the story which the author had dictated to his wife, and she read it through with unflagging interest. When she had come to the end at last she laid the magazine on the seat beside her and looked out of the window in front of her. But she did not see what was before her eyes—the high tenements, the enticing bar-rooms, the scrap of green square. She was not conscious of those who rode with her. She never noticed when her neighbors left the car, and when the vacant place on her right was taken by a small boy.

Her thoughts were over the hills and far away — over the hills of the years and far away in the past. A tale of youth and love, of bravery and manhood, had carried her back to her own brief love-story — to her own hero who had gone to the war a score of years before — who had gone and never come back. She lived over again that final parting with her young soldier-lover, whose unfound body was lying in a

nameless grave in a hollow of Malvern
Hill.

A sudden jolting of the car as a truck
crossed the track, and the little old maid
awoke from her day-dream. A glance at the
street told her that she had come too far,
and that she had passed the point where she
wished to alight full fifteen minutes before.
She signalled to the conductor to stop the
car again.

As she rose she recalled the story which
had thus entranced her, and she turned back
to the seat where she had left it. But it was
no longer there. The small boy had seen
his opportunity; he had seized it; and he
and the little old maid's copy of the midsummer number of *The Metropolis* had gone
off together.

She sighed, and then she smiled; and on
her way home on foot she stopped at a
news-stand and bought another copy for
the sake of the story she had read already.

IX.—ANOTHER READER.

In those days — for it was some sixteen years after the war that the story which the author had dictated to his wife was printed in the midsummer number of *The Metropolis* — there was a certain Indian reservation stretching for a hundred miles and more on each side of a great stream. Through the reservation and down this river one day towards the end of August there came floating a birch - bark canoe paddled by two stalwart Indians, and containing also two white men. They were young fellows, both of these, and they had come to spy out the land. They were engineers — the pioneers of civilization in the new West.

There had been heavy rains, and the river was high in its banks. A last shower had passed over them only an hour or so before. From the woods on each hand came the delicious fragrance of the forest after a rain, and a fresh breeze blew down with the current.

"How much farther is this blacksmith's ranch?" asked one of the young men, who had spent two years on the Pacific coast, where everything is a "ranch," from an orange grove to a hennery.

He was the elder of the two, a tall, hand-some young fellow; his companion was thick-set and red-haired.

The Indian paddling at the bow turned to his comrade in the stern and spoke a few words in his guttural vernacular, and when he had received a monosyllabic answer, more of a grunt than an articulate sound, he replied,

"Soon be there now. 'Bout a mile more, think."

"The sooner the better," the young engineer returned. "I sha'n't be sorry to get my head under a roof for one night, even if it doesn't rain again as it did last evening when we camped. There were times then when I thought the bottom had dropped out of the sky."

"Are you sure the blacksmith can take us in?" asked the other white man.

3

" Sure," replied the Indian, never pausing in his rhythmic paddling.

In the heart of the reservation there lived one white man, a blacksmith, paid by the United States Government to do such odd jobs as the Indians might desire. His cabin was high up on a bluff almost hidden by clustering trees from the eyes of the young engineers in the birch-bark even when their Indians ceased paddling and tied the canoe to the bank.

" Does he care for company ?" one of them asked, as the four men stepped out of the light craft.

" How ?" inquired the Indian who answered most of the many questions the young men were forever putting.

" Will he want to see us ?" said the white man, shaping his inquiry anew to suit the mind of the red man.

" Sure," the Indian replied. "Want to see me sure. I am brother of one of his wives."

" *One* of his wives ?" cried the Californian engineer. " How many wives has he, then?"

"Two now. Three once. One dead," was the sententious response.

" Oh !" said the engineer, thinking it best
to push his inquiry no further.

Although concealed from sight, the log-
cabin of the bigamist blacksmith was scarce
a hundred feet from the bank of the river.
Half-way up the Indian brother-in-law gave
a peculiar cry.

In less than a minute a young and rather
pretty Indian woman came flying down the
path in eager delight. A second and older
squaw also advanced to meet them, and offered to carry the guns the young men had
on their shoulders. The two engineers of
course refused, but the two Indians allowed
the women to relieve them of their burdens.

Brother and sister exchanged a few brief
sentences, and then the Indian turned and
said, " He home. He glad to see you."

And the blacksmith was glad to see them
—glad as only a white man can be who does
not gaze on a face of his own color a dozen
times a year.

" Come right in, boys," he cried, as soon
as he caught sight of them. " Come right
in an' make yerselves at home. I am, an'
I want ye should be. Put down yer traps,

and the women shall get ye somethin' to eat.
Ye won't be goin' on again this evening?"
he added, anxiously.

"Not if you'll keep us all night," answered
one of the young men.

"That's hearty," he responded, cordially.
"I'll keep ye a week ef only ye'll stay. It's
glad I am to see ye. These women o' mine
are sosherble enough—they're ez sosherble
ez they know how—but after all they ain't
white."

He was a large man, tall and generously
built; his voice was deep and full; his ample beard was streaked with gray, and so
was his shock of hair. He was perhaps
fifty years old.

"An' what might you two boys be a-doin'
here?" he asked, after he had made them
comfortable.

"We are engineers," one of them answered, "and we are—"

"Engineers, eh?" he interrupted. "Well,
I worked in a machine-shop myself once.
But what are ye doin' out here—there's no
engines out here?"

The young man who had been in Califor-

nia explained that, although they were employed by a railroad, they did not run a lo-
comotive.

He listened intently, but obviously failed
to understand.

"Well," he said at last, "whatever ye're
here for, ye're welcome. An' now we'll
have supper, and a snifter of old rye and a
pipe after it."

When they had finished supper the blacksmith pushed aside the largest log on the
hearth, and, taking up a burning stick, he
lighted his pipe and settled back for an
evening of enjoyment.

Unfortunately the two young men had
been kept up for several preceding nights,
and they were overburdened with sleep.
The warmth of the fire, the ample meal,
and the glass of liquor had weighted their
eyelids despite their desire to keep awake
for the sake of their host.

After he had been answered at random
once or twice, as one or the other of the engineers roused himself with an effort, the
blacksmith saw what the matter was.

"You two boys are sleepy," he cried,

"an' here I am, like a hog, a-keepin' ye up."

"We are a little drowsy, I confess," admitted one of them; "but we can sit up with you as long as you like."

"I allow I'd better get ye off to bed ez soon ez I can, or else I'll have to carry ye," he returned, mastering his disappointment with easy good-nature. "Here's the bunk the women have got fixed for ye; turn in now, an' turn out early in the mornin', an' we'll have a talk then."

The young men thanked him, and made ready for sleep. The old man stood over them as though there was something more that he wished to say. At last he remarked, in a deprecating way, "Ye haven't, either of ye, a paper ye could lend me overnight— a paper or a book? I ain't had anythin' to read for a mighty long while now. Ef ye've got anythin', let me have it now, an' I'll give it back to ye in the mornin'. I ain't sleepy to-night, an' I'll take it all in—ef ye've got anythin'."

The engineers felt in their pockets, and the young man who had been in California drew from his overcoat a copy of the midsummer number of *The Metropolis.*

"We haven't this morning's paper, I'm sorry to say," he answered, smiling, as he proffered the magazine, "but here's the last *Metropolis,* if you'd like to see it."

"*The Metropolis?*" queried the old man.

"It's a magazine," explained the engineer; "there are stories in it, and pictures, and all sorts of things."

"Thank ye," the blacksmith rejoined, as he took the thick pamphlet. "Pictures, eh? Well, I like pictures too. Sometimes these newspapers and books are chock full of long-tailed words that get away from me."

With that the young men bade him good-night, and as they turned into their bunk they saw him sitting by the fire with *The Metropolis* open in his hand.

And when they arose in the morning, there sat the blacksmith by the fire still grasping *The Metropolis,* still intent upon its pages.

When he saw them he got up and came forward.

"There's a power of good readin' in this

magaziny o' yours, an' there's one story there done me good to read."

The young man who had been in California pondered for a moment and then said, "The story with a fight in it?—the one about the sea-shore and the hill-side?"

"That's it," the blacksmith declared. "I ain't read any other, an' I don't want to—now. That's a story, that is, a real story, like the stories I used to hear as a boy—out of the Bible, mostly. I'd like to have met the man that fought that way."

"The hero of the story?" asked the inquirer.

"Well, he was a hero, for a fact," the old man responded; "he had sand in his craw, that fellow. He was a man ye could tie to. Of course the girl was true to him; she couldn't help it. A girl that wouldn't wait for a man like him wouldn't be no good."

This assertion was emphasized by a resounding slap on the thigh of the speaker.

"The editor of *The Metropolis* is my cousin," said the younger of the engineers. "I'll ask him to tell the author that his story has found appreciation out here in the back-woods."

"The author?" repeated the blacksmith. "That's the fellow who wrote it, eh? Well, he's a man, too! And he ain't any city fellow, either, I'll bet ye. He knows the woods too well for that. He's lived out-doors, he has."

Then the pretty little squaw appeared, and stood shyly before them.

"That means breakfast's ready, I reckon," said their host.

After they had broken their fast the young men lingered a while, smoking with the blacksmith and enjoying his talk.

When they were about to push off, the engineer who had been in California handed *The Metropolis* back to their host, saying, "I wish we had something better to leave with you to remember us by. But won't you keep this?"

"I'll take it, and thank ye," answered the blacksmith, heartily. "Now I can read that there story again."

X.—A READER OF ANOTHER SORT.

Early on the morning of the last day in August, in the huge yard outside of the rail-road station at Buffalo, two women were engaged in cleaning out a parlor-car which had arrived from New York late the night before, and which was to start on its return journey at ten o'clock that forenoon.

In a dark corner of the car, where the sleepy porter might easily overlook it, one of the women found a magazine. It was a worn and ragged copy of the midsummer number of *The Metropolis*. The woman took it to the window and turned its leaves with unintelligent looks.

"What's that ye have?" asked the other woman from the far end of the car, pausing a moment in her task of polishing the windows.

"It's a paper or a book, I don't know," responded the finder of the magazine. "It's pictures into it. I'll be takin' it home to the

boy. He do be wild now and then readin'
a piece in the paper."

This was said not without a certain maternal pride.

"An' can the boy read?" asked the other
cleaner, going back to her work.

"He can that!" responded the boy's mother, folding the magazine and thrusting it into
the huge pocket of her dress. "He reads as
fast and as easy as the teacher herself, and
him only going to school this six months."

"An' how old is the boy now?" inquired
the other, crossing over to polish the windows on the opposite side of the car.

"It's fourteen he'll be this next week,"
the mother replied. "He's the only one of
six that's left to me now, and it's a good lad
he is, too, barring a bit of wildness now and
then that he gets from his poor father."

And with that she went out on the plat-
form to polish the nickel-plated iron-work.
She was a woman of fifty or thereabouts,
good-natured and plain-featured, hard-work-
ing and worn by hard work.

When her long day's labor was over she
went home to her boy. They lived together

in two little rooms in a shanty over a grog-shop not far from the yard of the railroad. As she mounted the rickety stairs, she was surprised at the unwonted silence in the room that served them for kitchen. Generally the boy was home before her, and he had the fire started in the stove and the water in the kettle to boil; and often he came to the yard to meet her. When she entered the kitchen that last hot evening in August, when even the sunset breeze from the lake was sultry and feeble, there was no boy waiting for her, no fire laid, no water a-boiling.

But she had scarce taken off her bonnet when there was an eager footstep on the trembling stairs, and the boy broke into the room joyously.

"I couldn't help being late, mother," he cried; "I got a job from a gentleman down on Main Street, and he kept me till now. And, just think! He gave me half a dollar—a silver half-dollar, all in one piece."

And with that he took the coin from his pocket and tossed it in his mother's lap.

"It is a half-dollar, sure enough," said his

mother, after biting the edge of the coin with Old World caution.

"And this is Saturday night, mother," her son went on, hastily, "and you won't have to go to work till Monday, so I want you to spend part of this money for yourself, and get something good for to-morrow's dinner —a steak, for instance—a steak and onions ! You will, won't you, mother ?—just to please me ?"

The mother smiled back at him. "Well," she said, "I'll see what I can get when I do be going out the while."

"And I've got good news, too, mother," the boy continued. "I've got a place !—at least I think that I'm going to get one. The gentleman I did the errand for—he's a lawyer—asked me if I wanted a steady job, and I said yes, and I'm to go to his office on Monday at nine o'clock, and he'll see if I suit."

"That's good news, for a truth," she returned. "An' I've got something you'll be liking to see, too."

"What is it?" he cried, slipping his arm around her and kissing her.

She put her hand into her pocket and took out the magazine and handed it to him. " It's something to read," she said.

He opened it eagerly and turned the pages with delightful anticipations. " There's a lot of reading here, and I'll have such a good time a-reading it."

Seeing his ardent pleasure, the mother busied herself about the supper, lighting the fire in the stove and filling the kettle herself. When the meal was ready she called him ; for a moment he did not hear, so absorbed was he with the magazine.

" There's all sorts of good things in that book," he said, as he took his place at the table—" pictures, and poetry, and how a man sailed across the Pacific—don't they have big waves out there ! Ever so much bigger than I've seen on the lake ! There's stories, too. I'd just begun one of them. I picked it out because there was the picture of a fight in it, and I wanted to know which licked."

As soon as he had eaten his supper the boy lighted the little kerosene-lamp and sat down again at the story, losing himself in it at once, and becoming wholly oblivious of all things else.

The mother cleared off and washed up, and then went out to buy their Sunday's dinner with the money he had given her.

When she returned he was still intent on the story, and in a few minutes more he came breathlessly to the end.

"Oh, mother," he cried, "this is a splendid story! It's the best story I ever read!"

"Is it, lad?" she answered, wearily, but smiling.

"Sit down, and let me read it to you," he went on.

"Not to-night," she answered. "I'm that sleepy I couldn't listen to anything."

"To-morrow, then," he urged.

"To-morrow, if you like," she rejoined.

And when to-morrow came the boy read her the story as best he could, puzzled now and again by a chance polysyllable, but struggling through bravely.

"He do read beautiful," was the mother's comment, more interested in the reader than in what he was reading.

When he had made an end, and looked

up all aglow with enthusiasm, she said, " It's a fine story, no doubt."

" A fine story, mother?" he echoed. "It's great. It's true. That's the kind of man I'd like to be. That's the kind of man I mean to be, too."

" I hope you won't be fighting a duel then with swords, and getting killed."

"He wasn't killed," the boy retorted; "he killed the other man. And he didn't want to fight either, only he had to. He was a hero, that man. I can't fight, I suppose; but I can try to be as noble as he was, and as good."

" You are a good boy now," said his mother, kissing him.

On that Sunday afternoon the boy read the story again, for the third time, all to himself, and he made a solemn resolution to model himself on the hero. He felt as though the vision of that ideal would nerve him for the battle of life.

And so it came to pass. The boy went to the lawyer's office on Monday, and he stayed there till he grew to be a man. That story lingered fresh in his memory, and its

hero was as the young man's guardian
angel.

He developed true manliness, energy,
character, and ability. He became a lawyer himself, and on the death of the senior
partner of the firm to whose office he had
come as a boy he was taken into partner-
ship, although he was scarcely of age. Outside of his profession he broadened also and
grew in stature. At a time of trouble he
made himself the mouth-piece of the rail-
road men, whose claims he knew to be just,
though the directors of the company refused
to accede to them. To profit by the popu-
larity thus obtained his party nominated
him for the Assembly. By the advice of his
partners he accepted the nomination, and
by the help of the independent voters of
his district, by whom he was known and re-
spected, he was elected. His first thought
was for his mother ; he wished that she had
lived to see him thus honored by his fellow-
men ; he knew how happy and how proud
it would have made her.

The boy had grown to be a man, yet he
was the youngest member of the Assembly

4

that year; indeed, he was hardly old enough to vote. When he came to clear up his room before going to Albany, he found in the bottom of a drawer in his desk an old, worn, frayed magazine — the midsummer number of *The Metropolis* that his mother had brought home for him from the parlor-car. He sat down and read the story again, perhaps for the twentieth time; and he recognized again that it had been the inspiration of his life. Then there came to him a desire to tell the author all that the story had been to him, how it had moulded his whole life.

The boy went to New York as soon as time could be spared from the new duties at Albany and inquired for the author, only to find that he had died suddenly a fortnight after his story had been printed in the midsummer number of *The Metropolis*.

Then the boy, a boy no longer, sat down and wrote a long letter to the author's widow; and she thrilled with pleasure when she heard how her husband's last work had been as a lamp to a man's feet.

(1890.)

A CAMEO AND A PASTEL

A CAMEO AND A PASTEL

I. — THE CAMEO.

ROME, A. U. C. 722.

THE dining-room had been built apart from the house. It stood in the garden amid box-trees cut into threatening shapes of wild beasts, and beside a cypress clipped to suggest a dark green serpent coiling itself tightly about the brown trunk of the tree. With its white marble walls it crowned the brow of the hill that here sloped away to the bank of the placid brook below. It was open only to the north, but the westering sun shone through its windows, and left the long shadows of the tall poplars athwart the tessellated pavement. The twelfth hour of the day was near, and still the banquet was prolonged.

Upon the three wooden couches which formed three sides of a square in the centre of the room there reclined nine Romans— for the giver of the feast had borne in mind the saying of Varro that those invited should never be more in number than the Muses nor less than the Graces. Like his guests, the host had removed his shoes and his toga. He wore a light short-sleeved tunic, with the two broad perpendicular stripes of purple which denoted a knight. His face was dignified and kindly. His manner suggested that he was entertaining men of distinguished ability, but perhaps of inferior rank. He was crowned with a chaplet of dark ivy, not unbecoming to his closely cropped head.

The guests wore wreaths of roses upon their oiled locks, most of them, although one, whose white tunic bore the single dark stripe of a Senator, had preferred the crown of ivy leaves. The couches whereon they reclined were of wood thickly incrusted with ivory, and made easier by many cushions covered with light silks. The guests leaned on their left elbows, and ate with their right hands only. At the end of the course silent servants brought water in silver bowls and proffered linen napkins that the fingers might be washed, while another attendant wiped the low wooden table with a thick cloth.

In the open space before the table and the couches other slaves were casting down saffron-dyed sawdust, that it might absorb the blood which lay in little pools upon the pale pavement. There the gladiators had been fighting but a moment before, to entertain the guests at the banquet ; and having given strong proofs of their skill and of their courage, they had been dismissed, and were now behind the house, out of sight, one trying to stanch his wounds, the other stiff in death and carried by his comrades.

"This is a brave feast, Gaius Cilnius," said the guest who lay above the host on the couch at the right. "I have not had such good entertainment since that triumph of Cæsar when the Amazons contended with the lionesses."

"The Numidian did not fight ill," the host admitted.

"I never saw a more skilful stroke than

that with which he got under the guard of
the Gaul," returned the guest on the right,
a full-blooded, thick-necked man, with a face
hardened by exposure.

"He had as much strength as skill,"
added one of those who were reclining on
the couch on the left. "I saw his sword
come out at the back of the Gaul."

"A clean thrust, by Jove!" the first speaker rejoined; "and he gave it under dis-
advantage also, for the Gaul had already
cut off two of the fingers of his right
hand."

"Then it was a feat indeed!" said a young
man on the couch with the Senator; "a feat
worthy of commemoration in verse. And
we have three poets here now. Which of
you will immortalize the gladiator?"

"Publius Vergilius there," the ivy-crowned
Senator remarked, "is ever at work on his
epic. He carries it always on his mind, for
he has scarce said a word to us to-night,
from the egg to the apples."

The grave-visaged man whom he addressed
smiled tolerantly, and turning to the guest
at his side, he said, "Such a subject suits

rather the satire than the epic—eh, Quintus Horatius ?"

"There are those who would write an epic in twenty-four books on the life and adventures and death of a mouse," responded the guest thus invoked. "This afternoon at the bath, while I was anxious for my game of ball, there came a fellow who forced me to hear a long poem he had written yesterday while standing on one foot !"

"It is not enough to find a good subject," said the third poet, who was a young man with a faded expression; "we must also make sure of a publisher whose scribes will not betray us by their carelessness. My last elegy was sent forth with a thousand errors that the dullest slave should not have been allowed to make."

"I know nothing of scribes, Sextus Aurelius," the thick-necked man declared; "I like the sword and the spear more than the style. But it is indisputable that we have no such slaves as we used to have in the old days. The knaves are careless now and insolent. If I were a poet, and they

mangled my verses, I would have the blun-
dering rascals sent to frigid Mœsia ; they
would not make the same mistake twice."

" There are punishments nearer at hand,"
said the Senator, "and swifter.   When the
cook of Vedius Pollio three times failed to
stew the lampreys to his master's taste, the
fellow was thrown into the fish-pond, and I
doubt not that the lampreys found him to
their taste."

" There is no need thus to punish your
tricliniarch, Gaius Cilnius," declared the
poet with the serious face, as he helped
himself from the new dish the attendant
then presented.   " For here is a feast or-
dered to perfection.   The slave is worthy
of his master—is he not, Quintus Horatius ?"

" By Bacchus," replied the poet thus addressed, " he understands his art as well as
a Greek rhetorician understands the art of
speech.   He persuades us although we have
no appetite.   But the credit for his labors is
due to the friend who chose him."

" And the fellow is not to be praised for
this beaker of glass, red as the ruby and
as cunningly carved," the third poet inter-

posed; "nor for this silver cup," he added, taking the vessel from the hand of an attendant, who filled it to the brim with Falernian. "Is this the very goblet in which Cleopatra dissolved her pearl, when she drank to the health of Antony?"

The host smiled, and responded, "You have hit the mark with a chance arrow, Sextus Aurelius. That is indeed the goblet of Cleopatra. It was sent to me from Alexandria by the friend who bought me also the beakers of red glass."

The chief course of the dinner was now attained, and the slaves removed the tables from the room. The guests washed their hands again. Then there was silence for a little space, out of respect to the gods, while the salted meal was offered on the family altar, and while the libations of wine were poured solemnly upon the hearth to the sound of stately music.

When this ceremony had been duly performed, the second tables were brought in, with cakes of many kinds and all manner of fruits, while fresh snow was packed about the vessels containing the wine.

While the guests were enjoying the lighter dishes with which the banquet came to an end, a livelier strain of music swelled forth, as though some new entertainment was about to be presented.

"That is a Gaditanian air, if I mistake not," said the poet who had been addressed as Sextus Aurelius.

"Have you a dancer to show us?" asked the thick-necked man, with a certain suggestion of eagerness in his voice.

"Two," the host responded.

"Trust Gaius Cilnius to give us good measure," interjected one of the other poets.

"There are two Gaditanian girls, twin sisters, of whom report speaks favorably," the Senator remarked. "It is rumored that they have a perfect mastery of the strange dances of their own country. Even Cæsar commended them when they danced before him. Are these they?"

"They are the same," answered the host, modestly; "two Gaditanian slave girls. I have never seen them, but I thought it might interest you to compare their art with that of the dancers we have beheld so often in Rome."

"Nothing so helps digestion as to end a dinner with a dance," said Quintus Horatius, with a smile of humorous anticipation.

As the guests settled back on the couches to behold the sport at their ease, the host gave a signal, and the music swelled out again, with strange, broken rhythms.

Suddenly there sprang into the open space before the men two dark-eyed girls, one from each side of the broad portal. They met in the centre of the space, and grasped each other by the right hand and swung around, and then, as the music abruptly stopped, they stood still before the spectators, poised, each on one foot, in a graceful and captivating attitude. They were beautiful girls, both of them, scarce sixteen, lithe, slender, sinewy, with bronzed skins and thick dark hair. Their flowing garments, almost transparent, clung to their persons, falling in sweeping folds, but never reaching the saffron-dyed sawdust that covered the pale pavement.

Then, as the music struck up again, they

began to dance, swaying in time, retreating
one from the other, advancing with provo-
cation, keeping step faultlessly to the tune,
and bending their bodies in unison with the
enervating rhythm. A heightened color
came into the cheek of the thick-necked
guest, and the eyes of the Senator took on
a deeper glow.

Decorous at first, the sisters gained freedom as the dance went on, and with the
quickening music they added fervor to their
pantomime. So potent was the charm of
their motions that not a word was spoken,
while the dance rose to its climax with gestures as significant as they were graceful.
After a while the music slackened, and the
dance became more languorous, as though
the girls were caught up in a dream. Then,
with a sharp return of the former rapidity,
the dancers flashed across the slippery floor
again and were gone.

The Senator sank back on the couch,
while the poets and the other guests ap-
plauded. Then, while the servant whose
duty it was threw perfumes over the few
embers on the hearth, the diners made

ready for the symposium by casting dice to discover who should be king of the feast.

When the dancers withdrew, night was about to fall.   From the hut of a slave hidden in the hollow of the hill before the opening at the end of the dining-room a thin spiral of blue smoke curled softly upward in the darkening twilight, made visible by a final shaft of the expiring sunset.

II.—THE PASTEL.

NEW YORK, A.D. 1892.

Against the wall at the farther end of the studio hung a huge sheet, broad enough to have been taken from the great bed of Ware.   It was bleached by the hard glare of the limelight directed from the gallery at the back of the painter's workshop over the doorway leading to his smaller studio, where the supper was already set out.   Almost touching the pendent drapery, but a little to the left, were four chairs for the musicians who were to accompany the Spanish woman.

For the gyrations of the dancer a hollow semicircle of floor space had been left in front of the sheet, and bent rows of folding-chairs filled the rest of the long room. The carved coffers had been pushed back against the side walls under the worn tapestries and the tarnished embroidery of old altar-cloths. Vessels of brass, of copper, of baked clay, of delft, of twisted glass, stood on the larger cabinets. A panoply of arms, wherein could be seen a creese, a yataghan, an old flint-lock musket, a Springfield rifle, a bowie-knife, and two Arapaho arrows, was set on the wall over against a portrait of the owner of the studio, in Japanese costume, lovingly painted by a former pupil. There were other pictures here and there out of the way; and thrust in a corner on an easel, carefully hidden by a shabby velvet robe, was the unfinished portrait of one of the ladies who were giving the entertainment. Pendent from the ceiling by a cord was a stuffed sea-gull with outstretched wings, swaying softly to and fro as the floor trembled under the footsteps of the arriving guests.

It was nearly midnight, and for half an
hour or more the guests had been gathering,
greeting one another, and settling down in
little groups, until now the studio was beginning to be crowded, and the late-comers
found it hard to place themselves. Some
of those first to arrive had come leisurely
from betarded dinners, and some of those
last to arrive had come hurriedly from the
opera, hastening away before the tenor had
sung his death-song. They were all well
dressed, and they all seemed gay and eager
for amusement, with an air as of people out
in expectation of an unconventional entertainment. They were fairly representative
of the well-to-do dwellers in a great city.
Among them were many men and women
of fashion, some of them having no other
claim to distinction than the accident of
their social position, and some of them
leaders of society not only, but also in philan-
thropy and in citizenship. There were men
of letters, two or three essayists, three or
four novelists, and a poet or two. There
were artists, some of them friends of the
painter in whose studio the dance was to

5

take place. There was a clever young actor, with his pretty young wife. There were half a dozen statesmen—two of them high in the councils of the nation—who had come on from Washington specially to be present at the affair. There were pretty women a plenty, with diamonds agleam on their bosoms and in their hair. There was the thin young lady who had aroused public opinion against the dirty streets of the city; there was the young married woman who took time from society to do her duty as head of a school for the training of nurses; there was the plump widow who wrote clever articles on music and the drama; and there was the beautiful dark woman who had just been forced to seek a divorce from a brutal nobleman unable to appreciate her. There were young women and old who thought they had done their whole duty by the world when they looked charming and smiled at the compliments paid to them.

Above the chatter of many tongues could be heard the clear voice of one of the men from Washington, who had once been an attaché in Madrid. "Why is she so late, this Andalusian caperer?"

"She doesn't finish at the theatre till nearly eleven," said the handsome woman to whom he had spoken; "but she promised to dance as little as she could this evening and to take no encores, so as to save herself fresh for us."

A novelist who had just arrived from Italy leaned over and asked the young lady by his side, "It's a new act, isn't it, this hav-ing a dancer come here at midnight to give a private performance?"

"She's done it two or three times for us this winter," the young lady answered. "You know the theatre where she appears is so common that we can't go there; and so, you see, if she didn't come to a studio now and then, why, nobody would see her."

Then there was a sudden parting of the little group of men gathered about one of the hostesses near the door. Four musi-cians entered and took the seats reserved for them. They were swarthy and dark-eyed; one of them was a fine-looking fellow with a shrewd smile hovering about his sensual mouth. He was the leader, and played the guitar; his companions had, one a man-dolin, and two of them violins. With the appearance of the musicians there was an instant stir all over the studio, and people settled into their places and made room for one another, and turned their attention to the coming entertainment. The young men who had been standing inside the reserved semicircle, bending over and chatting with the ladies on the front row, now squatted on the floor and sat cross-legged.

The hush of expectancy was broken as the dancer entered, walking with a free and feline tread. Amid loud applause, clapping of hands, and tapping of fan sticks, she took the seat that had been set for her in the centre of the open space, close to the sheet, against which her black shadow was cut out boldly by the limelight that now bright-ened. She sat still for a few seconds, until the musicians struck up a wailing and riot-ous rhythm. She threw back her scarf and arose from her chair. The music swelled languorously and louder, and then she began to dance, coming forward a little, until by

"THE MUSIC SWELLED, AND SHE BEGAN TO DANCE"

chance her shadow was under the shadow
of the bird with outstretched wings.

She was a daringly handsome woman, of
superb health, of intense vitality, of unfailing grace, of undeniable charm—due not
only to the dark deep eyes, made darker
and deeper by kohl lines below and above,
and not only to the full red lips and the
dazzling white teeth they revealed when
they parted; not only to the flash of the
glance even, nor to the sudden delight of
the smile; but rather to some intangible,
invisible, indisputable potency of sex which
lent irresistible fascination to irregular features.   In repose the face was heavy and
sad; but a smile transfigured it almost beyond recognition.   It was a Spanish face,
no doubt, but with more than a hint of the
gypsy or of the Moor.   The neck and arms,
more decorously covered than those of most
of the ladies who were looking on, were
browned, and the thick fingers of both
hands were encased with a dozen diamond
rings.   Her dress, which fell a little below
the knee, was of yellow satin, decked with
an abundance of black lace.   She wore a

rose in the heavy braids of her midnight hair.

Her dance was like her beauty, irregular and irresistible. It was Spanish in essence, perhaps gypsy at times, with haunting memories of the Orient. It began with a Moorish swaying of the body and a bold swing of the hips, preceding a few simple steps to the right and to the left, a few bending turns, now one way and now the other, taken with easy flexibility, in strict time to the lilt of the tune the musicians kept playing. Often the suppleness of the torso was as important as the swiftness of the feet. It was a strange and startling performance, and its fascination was as strange as the dancer herself. As a dance it was voluptuous, and yet decent; full of suggestion to some, and yet devoid of offence to all who were ignorant as to the symbolic possibilities of primitive pantomime. As it went on, the ladies watched it with eager enjoyment, following every movement of arm, of body, and of foot. The men leaned forward with a tenser interest, with a gaze that never relaxed, and sometimes with a tightened

breathing. At any unexpected twist of
the dancer's body or unusually artful feat
there were incipient cheers and loud cries
of " Ollè !"

At last the music died away and the dancing ceased. She bowed again and again as
the plaudits rang out, accepting them with
a hesitancy that seemed almost shy. Then
she sat down, breathless and hot. Two or
three of the men who had been sitting on
the floor on the front line of spectators got
on their feet and went forward with compliments, which she received with purely professional gratitude. She accepted congrat-
ulations on her skill with a heartiness which
was perhaps perfunctory. In repose the expression of her countenance was almost
sombre, until it was illuminated by her
swift smile.

The guests who had seen her before
compared this performance with those preceding. One young man informed a young
girl that she did not dance as freely as she
used. "You see, some fellow told her she
had heart-disease, so she spares herself now.
I always sing out 'Ollè !' as loud as I can,

and as óften too, to try and get her excited a little and to keep her up to her work."

"I think some of the married women might go up and talk to her," said the young lady; "she looks so timid I feel almost as if I ought to get presented to her, so as to encourage her a little."

Side by side at the rear of the studio, standing clear of the last row of chairs, were a poet and a novelist.

"Do you suppose she really cares for the applause and the compliments," asked the novelist, "or is that brilliant smile of hers part of the performance?"

"I don't know," the poet responded. "She seems to take to it kindly. Do you see how she turns again and again to that mandolin-player at her right, and how he looks at her with a calm air of proprietorship?"

"Oh yes," the novelist returned; "they say he's her husband—but then they will say anything."

Then the music started again, a low, throbbing, pathetic air this time, and as some of the audience recognized it, there was an outbreak of applause. The Spaniard arose and put on a black felt hat, which she pulled down over her eyebrows, and she reached down and picked up a long cane or pilgrim's staff. The dancer was now to appear as a singer. The song was simple and dramatic; and the singing was varied by much pantomime, by an attempt to express its emotion histrionically, by an obvious theatric effort. The end of every stanza brought an odd little chorus, to the notes of which the performer walked in time with an indescribable swagger, irredeemably common, but never vulgar in the lower sense of the word. At the end of the final stanza the music was prolonged, and the walk around became a dance, like the first and yet unlike it, not the same and yet a variation of the same theme. It had more freedom than its predecessor and a wilder abandon, as if the gypsy or the Moor was overpowering the Spaniard. As it went on there were frequent clappings of hands and shouts of " Ollè," as though the spectators also were waking up.

The young man who had been talking to

the young lady found himself by the side of
the visitor from Washington who had once
been an attaché at Madrid.

"I suppose you have seen better than
this in Spain?" he asked, doubtfully.

"I have seen much the same thing," was
the answer. "Nothing more graceful; nothing more fascinating."

"Ah, but you just wait till after supper,"
cried the young man, enthusiastically.

The poet overheard this, and moved away.
He delighted in the light and the color of
the thing, in its movement and rhythm, in
the aroma of luxury, in the unconvention-
ality of the entertainment; but his conscience smote him.

"Do you see the shadow of that bird,"
asked the novelist, "descending on the
dancer like a spirit of purity? And if you
will look over here at the right of the drapery, you can catch sight of the death-mask
of Shakespeare looking on at these revels•
with sightless eyes as if he enjoyed them.

"I feel like a barbarian of the lower em-
pire," the poet responded. "I shall be
ready soon for the gladiators, and I don't

doubt I should hesitate whether to turn my thumb down or not."

The music ceased suddenly, and the dancer, after bowing once and again, dropped into her chair, visibly panting. Two ladies went forward together to express their pleasure at her performance. The young man who accompanied them borrowed one of their fans, and sinking on his knees by the side of the dancer, he began to fan her.

(1892.)

TWO LETTERS

TWO LETTERS

FROM THE "GOTHAM GAZETTE" OF APRIL 21.

FROM AN OCCASIONAL CORRESPONDENT.

GEORGETOWN, DEMERARA, *April* 1.

I ARRIVED here last Sunday, safe and sound, and I expect to be able to proceed shortly to the scene of the boundary dispute between England and Venezuela. I have heard of a boat sailing next week for the mouth of the Orinoco, on which I hope to secure a passage. Although there has been a fortnight or so of pleasant weather, the rainy reason is not yet over, and travelling is not altogether as easy or as pleasant as it might be.

I cannot say that I regret the delay, as it has enabled me to make acquaintance here with a few charming people, from whom I expect to take useful letters when I go on my journey.

For another reason also I am not dissatisfied that I have been forced to remain in this hospitable town. The delay has given me an opportunity to make the acquaintance of Mr. Walter Stead, an American citizen of English birth, and a man of singular courage and nobility of character. It has enabled me also to secure from Mr. Stead's own mouth a full and exact account of the extraordinary attack recently made upon him in the interior, up the Essequibo River. Although Mr. Stead, like other men of positive convictions and unhesitating boldness, has not a few enemies here, I find that there is a general agreement of opinion that the outrage on him should be carefully investigated, and that condign punishment should be meted out to the survivors of the strange people against whom he has had to defend himself. That any portion of the treasure he risked his life to protect can now be recovered is extremely doubtful.

Mr. Stead came to British Guiana as a

representative of the Essequibo Gold Company, an American organization, of which Mr. Samuel Sargent is president. Although the mines have never received adequate attention, it has been known for centuries that there was gold in abundance in the mountains of Guiana.

It was in this country that Sir Walter Raleigh placed his El Dorado, following in this the belief of the earlier Spaniards; and when Choiseul sent out his 12,000 colonists here in 1763, it was hoped that they would be able to develop the gold mines; but so great was the mortality consequent on bad management that within five years after the arrival of this colony barely a thousand survived. The insalubrity of the climate has been partly to blame for this neglect of the golden treasure which lies almost within man's grasp. And at one time the fear of the Indians was also a deterrent. As is well known, the Caribs were cannibals; now they have mostly died out. The Araucans are natives of high intelligence and unusual courage. Not a few of the bush tribes retain flitting traces of their former Christian-

6

ity, which now commingles with their degraded superstitions. In the mountains at the head of the Essequibo there has been rumored to be a tribe of White Indians, who were supposed to be the last of the ancient Peruvians, living to-day as their ancestors lived under the Incas when the Spaniards conquered the country. That such a tribe still exists has hitherto been but a doubtful rumor, as no white man had ever succeeded in penetrating into their country. But to-day, although we know little more about them, we know at least that such a tribe does exist. Mr. Walter Stead has good reason to remember them, and it is the tale of his misadventures in their country that I shall try to tell in this letter, regretting only that my feeble pen cannot reproduce adequately the stirring accents of Mr. Stead's story as I heard it from his own lips.

I must begin by saying that although it has been well known for centuries that there was abundant gold in the mountains where the many rivers which traverse Guiana have their source, hitherto the attempts to get at it have been spasmodic and more or less unsatisfactory. In the upper waters of the Caroni, in Venezuela, and at Arataya, in Dutch Guiana, the prospector has been fairly successful, and many a bag of golden dust has rewarded his enterprise. But it was not until a strong syndicate of Americans, headed by Mr. Samuel Sargent, organized the Essequibo Gold Company that any serious endeavor was made to wrest the precious metal from the heart of the Sierra Acarai Mountains.

The Essequibo Gold Company, supported by abundant capital, was able to make a careful survey of the situation. Its agents skilfully prospected throughout the length and breadth of British Guiana. The reports they sent home were compared, and the specimens of ore they forwarded were assayed; and the consensus of expert opinion was to the effect that it would be best to begin operations almost at the head of the Essequibo water-shed, between the Zibingatzako Pass and Mount Turako. Two years ago a body of experienced Californian miners was got together and despatched to Demerara, whence the men, with their tools, were sent up the Essequibo as far as the King William IV. Cataract. Hence they had still to push their way into the tropical wilderness nearly a hundred miles farther, through the territory of the friendly tribe of the Taruma Indians.

For now eighteen months these resolute Americans have been hard at work digging gold from the flanks of the Sierra Acarai. It has hitherto been impossible to provide these sturdy miners with the improved machinery to which they have been accustomed. Hydraulic mining, for example, has not yet been attempted. Although the enterprise has passed the experimental stage, the works are still of the most primitive character. Yet the results have been very encouraging, and the yield of gold is steadily increasing. The facilities of approach have been improved, although they are still wholly inadequate. A monthly messenger descends from the miners to Demerara; the products of the washings come down every quarter; and supplies and reinforcements are sent up from the coast at least twice a year. In the organization of these means of communication Mr. Stead has been invaluable. For a year he has been here, going to and fro, acquainting himself with every detail of the work, and devising improved methods for its accomplishment. And it was in pursuance of this duty that he met with misfortune, and was forced to fight for his life.

Before setting forth the details of his brave struggle—one man against many—I ought, perhaps, to try to set before you the man himself. At first sight he does not seem to be cast in heroic mould. He is shorter than, the average, and his figure is slim rather than sturdy. But, slight as he is, he is wiry and tough; and his meagre form sheathes a soul as noble as any in the breast of a Crusader of old. Although Mr. Stead is not yet forty, his hair, a rich bronze, is already beginning to be streaked with gray, and the deep lines on his thin face tell the same tale of hard battling with the vicissitudes of life. His eyes are restless and yet piercing. His expression is self-reliant; one does not hesitate to say at first sight, " Here is a shrewd man, able to take care of himself." And when occasion serves, Mr. Stead is able to take care of himself, as I shall show.

Mr. Stead reached the mines some two months ago, bearing letters and instructions. The superintendent of the company's works there was beginning to get a little uneasy about the accumulated gold, which was increasing with unexpected rapidity, and yet he was not able to send down a detachment of men to guard the treasure to the coast. There were rumors of uneasiness among the surviving Caribs, perhaps the most dangerous of the Indian tribes, and a friendly Taruma had come into the camp with a strange story about some marauding expedition of the alleged tribe of White Indians, whose possible identity with the surviving people of the Incas I have already recorded. That such a tribe even existed has hitherto been doubtful, and the superintendent, although he was not a little alarmed by the reports, which came to him from two or three sources, was not at all convinced either that these Inca Indians were on the war-path, or even that there was any such tribe. Nevertheless, when the time came for Mr. Stead's departure, and he offered to bear down to the coast as much gold-dust as he could carry in a belt around his waist, the superintendent accepted his proposal gladly. Although spare, as I have said, Mr. Stead is a man of unusual strength, and he was able to bestow on his person about forty pounds' weight of gold, worth approximately ten thousand dollars. The flat ingots of the precious metal were sewed into a broad belt or jacket, girt tightly about the waist, and supported by straps over the shoulders. This jacket-belt was made for him by a native woman.

For the most part the long and wearisome journey was to be made in a canoe, and the burden of the gold was therefore far less than it would have been had it been necessary for Mr. Stead to cover the distance on foot.

The bearer of the treasure was amply armed. He carried a repeating rifle, and he wore a revolver at his waist. He was to be accompanied throughout his trip by one white man, and one only. This companion was a fellow-employé of the Essequibo

Gold Company, Mr. Thomas Austin, also an American, but a man of far less readiness of resource and strength of character than Mr. Stead. Austin had occupied a humble position in the service of the company, and the climate had broken his health, so that he begged the privilege of returning to Demerara with Mr. Stead, to whose recommendation, indeed, he owed his engagement.

The canoe which was to bear the intrepid travellers on their long and lonesome voyage was of the kind called by the natives a "wood-skin"—that is to say, it was made from the heavy bark of the purple-heart; it was about fifteen feet long, and it could carry comfortably the two voyagers, with a supply of provisions sufficient for their journey.

On the first stage of the journey, down to the King William IV. Falls, the two Americans were accompanied by a band of the friendly Tarumas; but after assisting Mr. Stead and his companion over the portage around the falls, these Indians bade them farewell, and returned to their own country, not daring to venture into the wild-

er Carib territory, through which the Essequibo River passes. Mr. Stead is now inclined to believe that the Tarumas were
also affrighted by the rumors about the
White Indians.

This passage through the land of the
Caribs was always accounted the most dangerous part of the voyage down the river
from the mines to the coast. Mr. Stead and
Austin accomplished it without delay or
mishap. For hours they floated down with
the swollen current, making no other exer-
tion than was needed to keep the canoe in
the swiftest channel. For hours they sped
along in the midst of the oppressive silence
of a South-American forest—a vast and
deadly stillness, awful beyond belief, and
broken only now and again by a startling
scream. At noon sometimes a booming
crash would echo through the forest, followed by a clang like that of an iron bar
against a hollow tree. Then the silence
would settle down again, and it might be an
hour or more before a piercing half human
and wholly terrible shriek would shrill out.
Towards night, again, as the twilight fell

and the long shadows of the twisted trees
lay black and contorted on the water, a cry
would suddenly rend the air—a weird, blood-
curdling yell; and the travellers would tire
themselves in vain effort to account for it.
And through these horrible sounds, and
through this still more horrible silence, the
two Americans fared forward to the settlements of civilization on the coast.

Through the territory of the Caribs they
passed without adventure or misadventure.
It was not until they came under the shadow of the Makarapan Mountains that they
had the first suggestion of impending evil.
They landed for dinner on the left-hand
side of the stream, and as they were about
to prepare their simple repast there appeared
before them suddenly three stalwart warriors. Fortunately Mr. Stead saw them re-
flected on the surface of a pool of water
spreading from a bubbling spring beside
which the travellers had seated themselves,
and he was able to grasp his repeating rifle
in time to confront the strange visitors.
Apparently the new-comers knew what fire-
arms were, although they themselves were

equipped only with bows and arrows. They advanced and stood before the two Americans. Mr. Stead stared at them in surprise, as he saw how they differed from the ordinary native of the Essequibo Valley. The Indians of Guiana adorn their bodies in fantastic patterns, with a red paint which is highly scented, and they wear necklaces of boars' teeth. The three men who stood before Stead were unpainted, and they wore only ornaments of feathers ; and, most remarkable of all, their skins, although not white, were far lighter in color than any Indian's.

For a moment the two groups stood silently facing one another. Then the White Indians, as Mr. Stead calls them, drew nearer, and the one who seemed to be their leader spoke. Austin, who had been longer in South America than Stead, said that the only word he could recognize was "gold." At first this seemed to have no significance, but when the chief approached Stead, and touched the treasure-belt he wore beneath his shirt, and sought to remove it, then the Americans knew that the White Indians were aware of the object of their journey, and that thereafter they might have to defend the gold with their lives. How the Indians got wind of the precious belt it was impossible to say, but Mr. Stead has reason to suspect that one of the Taruma Indians —perhaps the husband of the woman who had made his treasure-belt—spied out the secret, and managed to communicate it to the men who now sought to waylay him. When the White Indian reached out for the belt, Mr. Stead sternly thrust off the fellow's hand, and with energetic gestures indicated that the treasure was his, and that it could not be surrendered. Among most savage races sign-language is highly developed, and the three men who stood before Stead obviously understood his emphatic negation. They made another vain effort, and then they withdrew into the heavy woods which spread away from the river on both sides.

At Mr. Stead's suggestion, the two Americans hastily reloaded their canoe, and dropped down the river a dozen miles or more, stopping at last on the other side at a bend of the stream, where there seemed to be a level space of grass. Here they made a hasty meal, having started a fire at the roots of a withered cotton-wood tree which stood in the centre of the clearing.

Around this tree the ground seemed to have been carefully cleared, and at a distance of a dozen yards or so there was a-circle of white stones, so regularly placed that it was scarcely possible not to accept them as having been arranged by human hands. Throughout Guiana the huge cotton-wood decays into fantastic shapes like the skeleton of a demon. Austin told his companion that the natives are very superstitious about the cotton-wood, and will never cut one down, or even throw stones at it, believing that misfortune will surely follow if they do. Many are the strange beliefs among the Indians. "There is even known to be a tribe," said Austin, "which worships a sacred bird." Mr. Stead recalled the custom of the Incas in the old days of Peruvian civilization, when the monarch wore upright in his turban three feathers of a rare and curious bird, the coraquenque. This biped was sacred to the ruler; it served only to supply the plume which was the badge of sovereignty; and if an ordinary citizen killed one the penalty was death.

The two Americans had built their fire in the prickly spurs of the tree, feeding it with chips from the withered branches, which still extended from the hollow trunk. When they were finishing their repast the fire had burned well into the roots, and the whole tree began to blaze up. As the smoke poured thick through the rotten trunk, as through a chimney, there was a noise of wings and a weird hooting, and an awkward fowl flew up out of the hollow, where it had been reposing.

Obeying a sudden impulse, Stead seized his gun, and as the fleeting object was outlined against the fading twilight, he fired, and brought it down with a single shot.

" Let's hope I haven't killed the sacred bird !" he cried, as the gory mass of feathers fell to the ground.

But that was exactly what he had unwittingly done; and the evil deed brought dire misfortune. As the echo of the shot died away, the two Americans heard a long loud whistle almost human, but with a ghoulish shrillness.

" Now we shall have bad luck," said Austin, shivering despite the fire before which he was standing.

" Why?" asked Stead.

" Because that is the call of the Didi, and it always forebodes evil to those who hear it."

Mr. Stead was aware that the Didi is an unknown and unseen evil spirit, which the natives believe to lurk in the dark depths of the forest. To him is attributed any sudden death or mysterious disappearance. But Mr. Stead is not superstitious ; laughing lightly at Austin's evident dread, he stepped into the brush and brought forth the body of the bird.

" It is like the coraquenque," he said, as he held it in his hand. " See, here are the three royal feathers."

" Hush !" whispered Austin, suddenly, gripping his arm. " We have been followed. Don't you hear the paddles?"

Stead listened intently, and from the distance there came a succession of faint sounds.

" They are on our trail," said Austin.

" Who ?" asked Stead.

" The White Indians," answered Austin. " They know that you have the gold, and they will not cease from following us till they get it. Don't you hear them ?"

Again the two Americans held their breath as they bent forward listening. From over the water there came a regular rhythmical sound as of paddle strokes. Then suddenly there rang out again the shrill, uncanny whistle of the Didi.

" I'm going to get out of this," cried Austin.

Mr. Stead threw down the body of the bird. " If there is some one on our track," he said, " we had best not stand in the glare of this fire. Nobody could ask a better mark than we are here."

They stepped back into the shadow. Fortunately they had not unloaded the woodskin, and Mr. Stead had not removed the treasure-belt from his waist. Their canoe was hidden in the shrubbery which thickly fringed the river a few yards below the point where they had lighted their fire. When they came to the wood-skin, night was already settling down on them. Only the blazing tree cast a ruddy glow.

Austin got into the boat at once; but Stead, after handing his rifle to his companion, stood on the shore, hidden in the darkness, peering forward to see if they were really pursued.

"Come on," cried Austin; "we are losing time."

"Why need we go?" said Stead. "I want first to make sure that there is a reason for flight."

"Reason enough," Austin answered. "If you had been in this country as long as I, you would know that the Didi never brought anybody good-luck."

Stead did not answer. At that instant he saw the bow of a canoe come out of the shadow into the light of the flaming cottonwood.

There were three men in this canoe; two of them were paddling, and one was seated in the centre. They were the three White Indians who had visited the two Americans in the afternoon.

7

"What are you waiting for *now?*" Austin whispered, in a trembling voice. "You see they *are* after us. Get into the boat at once, and we can still escape them."

Stead looked at his companion with some slight surprise. "I don't think," he said, "that two Americans ought to run away from three Indians."

"But we don't know how many more they have coming with them," answered Austin, pettishly. "Enough of this foolishness, I say. Get in now, or I'll push off without you."

Stead said nothing, but silently watched the three men make fast their canoe and step out on land. They looked up the river, and one of them gave a doleful cry. It was repeated from far over the water, and then taken up again and again, farther and farther off.

"They have a dozen more wood-skins on the way down here," said the timorous Austin. "I give you fair warning I am not going to stay here to count them. With you or without you, I'm off."

Before Stead could reply, a second canoe

came in sight. As it touched the bank, five more of the White Indians alighted from it. The three who had first landed drew near to the tree on fire. One of these almost stepped on the carcass of the bird Stead had shot. He stopped and picked it up, and gave a sudden wail of sorrow. The others had no sooner laid eyes on the slain bird, with its sacred feathers bedraggled with blood, than they too made a pitiful cry. Then, as the new-comers approached, the bird was pointed out, and all eight of the White Indians raised a fierce yell. Though the language was unknown, the meaning of their outcry was plain enough—they would seek revenge for this sacrilege. And so, by his innocent shot, Mr. Stead had added a religious fervor to their pursuit; and they sought now not only his treasure, but his life as well.

Brave as he was, he felt that the time had come to withdraw. But when he turned to join Austin in the wood-skin, he found that it was gone. Affrighted by the revengeful shriek, Austin had deserted him. Mr. Stead was alone, without a friend, without a boat, without food. He had nothing but his treasure-belt and his revolver, with the twenty or thirty cartridges he happened to have on his person.

At this moment a third canoe appeared, and five more White Indians were added to the group gathered about the fire. Mr. Stead took advantage of the noise and excitement which arose among his foes as they showed the new-comers the body of the bird he had slain, and crept farther back into the bushes as noiselessly as he could. Escape by way of the river was impossible, now that Austin had abandoned him. To get away from the water into the woods which masked the hills was his sole chance of safety. For the moment the one thing needful was to take himself out of sight of the rapidly increasing band of White Indians, who were determined to kill him, moved now by the double motive of avenging a sacrilege and of plundering his treasure. After he might get clear of them, it would be time enough to make plans for returning to the settlements of civilization.

With every muscle at its highest tension, Mr. Stead wormed his way along the ground, borne down by the weight of his gold, which even then, in the dire extremity of his danger, he did not think of abandoning. Inch by inch, foot by foot, he crawled away from the fatal spot. At every step he expected to betray himself. Every minute he feared to see the White Indians scatter in pursuit of him. To this day he does not know why they made no immediate effort to discover his whereabouts. The shot that killed the coraquenque was fired when they were in hearing, but two minutes before they came in sight, and the bird must yet have been warm with life when they took it in their hands. Why it was that they did not make an instant search for the man, who could not have been far off, is to him inexplicable. Mr. Stead is now inclined to accept this dilatoriness and delay of his enemies as the providential means of his escape. As it was, he succeeded in gaining the verge of the denser forest on the hill-side just as the moon came out and flooded with light the vacant spaces across which he had fled but a few minutes before under cover of the friendly darkness.

The hill forest was distant barely half a mile from the river-bank, but Mr. Stead had taken more than an hour to make the journey, on his hands and knees mostly, except where he arose to dash across a clearing as swiftly as he could. He sat him down in the shadow of the trees, to take breath and to collect his thoughts. He had only a vague idea as to his exact position, but he believed that a little way below the mountain rose abruptly on each side of the stream, and the river ran through a narrow gorge. On the other side, it might be some ten or twenty miles away, or it might be more, there was a village of friendly Indians, where he had once spent the night on his journey upstream to the gold mines. If he could but get to this village he doubted not that he could procure a wood-skin and assistance to continue his journey to the coast, where he had agreed to deliver the treasure which now weighed him down.

The blazing tree by whose roots he was standing when he had shot the fatal coraquenque a couple of hours before had burned itself out, but on the open space before it there was gathered a group of the White Indians which he reckoned to contain at least fifty. They were drawn up in rings about the chief—the tall man who had first addressed Stead — and this chief seemed to be haranguing them. A cry of approval punctuated his sentences, and when he concluded there arose a yell of vengeance, which Mr. Stead, alone in the darkness of the hill forest above them, could hear, and heard without fear.

Yet it was with a certain beating of the heart that he saw his foes scatter in search of him at last. While he was recovering his breath and resting his muscles, a shout from the shore notified him that the point was discovered where the canoe had been made fast. The trail of Mr. Stead's tortuous and crawling progress from that spot into the denser brushwood fifty yards away was plain. In fifteen minutes more the White Indians in a compact body were pressing forward on his track through the undergrowth of the foot-hills.

Then began for Mr. Stead a flight by night which was enough to break the nerves of the bravest of men. Through the darkness, in the forest, uphill and on the level, lighted only by the chance rays of the moon as they broke through the heavy foliage, borne down by the weight of his golden burden, worn out by the labor of the day and by the haste of his escape, on and on he toiled, hearing the call of his pursuers, now fainter and now louder, pushing ahead, but not knowing where he was going, and conscious finally of naught but a struggle between his love of life and an overmastering fatigue, which multiplied with every step he took.

At last he could do no more. He had been climbing higher and higher, and he had come out on a shelf of rock, from which the mountains seemed to rise sheer before him. He had no strength to advance, even if his benumbed intelligence could see a path upward. He sank down where he stood, exhausted absolutely, conscious only that the signals of his pursuers had been fainter of late. But before he could even formulate a hope that he had distanced them, or that they had lost his trail,

Nature claimed her own, and he was asleep.

How long he slept he did not know; but when he awoke the sun was breaking over the mountains. He lay still, slowly collecting his thoughts. Even then he could not recall all the incidents of his flight. He had fled, and they had pursued, and he was safe so far—this was all he knew, and it was almost all he cared. How he was to advance farther he did not know, or what he was to do next. His bones ached as he lay there on the ground, his mouth was parched, and he began to feel the pangs of hunger. He looked about him to see if he could not find some fruit with which he might stay his stomach, or a brook whereat he might quench his thirst. He was lying on a ledge of rock but thinly covered with earth, although richly robed with the luxuriant vegetation of the tropics. In front of him rose the sheer cliff which in the darkness had barred his farther progress. It was this rock, an unsurmountable obstacle in the darkness, which was now to prove a means of safety by day.

As Mr. Stead gazed about him in search of what might serve as meat and drink, the light of dawn strengthened, and the precipice which towered before him began to glow with the beams of the rising sun. In this increase of light he seemed to see a strange medley of figures moving across the face of the rock. At first he mistrusted his senses, feeling that his fatigue had perhaps made him subject to hallucinations or visions. But as he looked again he found that his eyes had only half deceived him. The figures were there before him, but they were motionless. Carved on the face of the cliff in rude relief, they were colored into a semblance of reality.

Then Mr. Stead knew where he was. He recognized the fact that he had before him one of the Pictured Rocks of the Essequibo, which many a voyager had sought and very few had ever found. He had been told that they existed in three or four places, and that they were always so situated that they could be seen from afar by the first rays of the rising sun. What their origin might be, nobody can declare with precision.

Sometimes they are apparently commemorative of some royal hero or some noble feat at arms ; sometimes they are obviously explanatory devices designed to guide the wayfarer.

That which Mr. Stead was fortunate enough to find before him belonged to this latter class. It served as a sign-post, as it were, to a way of safety. In this case the tinted sculptures indicated a sort of profile map of the mountains, with the river flowing between. An outstretched hand with pointing finger showed the direction to be taken if the traveller desired to pass over to the other side of the stream by a hanging bridge which swung across the chasm. Rudely cut figures as rudely daubed with color were proceeding along the paths and passing over the frail bridge. Then Mr. Stead remembered that on the journey up the river they had had to make a long portage around the mountain because the stream here ran between high walls, and was not to be ascended by boat on account of its succession of rapids and cataracts. He had never heard that there was any such bridge across the river as was seen in the picture-writing, but there might very well be. And if there were, then he had at least a chance of escape. Once across the river, he thought he could find his way to the village of friendly Indians a few miles farther below; then the rest of the journey would be easy and without danger.

How distant the bridge might be, if indeed there were any bridge, he could not estimate from the pictorial outlines before him. But whatever was the distance the direction was plain, and the journey must be undertaken. Mr. Stead arose and tightened the belt around him. Following the suggestion of the outstretched finger, he started along the ledge of the cliff, and now that full daylight helped him, he soon came to a break in the rock above him — a break through which it was easy to attain the brow of the mountain. Here he came out on a table-land less densely covered with vegetation. Although almost level, it sloped gently upward. A quarter of a mile away to his right the ground broke, and here he supposed the high bank of the river to be.

A mile beyond him, or it might be two, the cliff of the opposite river-bank rose up, and apparently the channel narrowed. There, if anywhere, would be the bridge which was figured in the picture-writing.

Hitherto Mr. Stead had proceeded very cautiously, feeling his way lest he should walk into an ambush, looking back often to make sure that he was not followed, and keeping his revolver in his hand, with his finger on the trigger. But in the joy of seeing the table-land stretch away before him, with the hope that the bridge of safety was but a mile or two ahead, inadvertently he paused for a moment at the edge of the cliff up which he had climbed. For a few seconds only was his figure outlined against the sky.

Brief as was this space of time it sufficed. A cry arose from the hill-side beneath him to the left of the path by which he had come; it was the same cry with which the White Indians in the first canoe had called to their comrades in the other boats. Instantly it was repeated—first to the right of him, then again to the left, then four or

five times farther down the hill-side. There
was no mistaking the meaning of these
calls: he was discovered, and the enemy
was on his trail.

Mr. Stead looked over the cliff again.
Not one of the White Indians was in sight.
So he knew he had a good start. To stand
still was but to invite death. His one
chance of life lay in reaching the bridge
first. He set off at once at a rapid pace
notwithstanding the heavy weight of treasure which lined his belt. If it were absolutely necessary to save his life, he was
ready to abandon the gold, but only under
the most desperate circumstances did he in-
tend to give it up. The pursuers meant to
kill him and to get his precious burden;
and Mr. Stead was resolved to prevent, if
he could, their doing either.

Knowing that his enemies were now following him closely, he looked back with
every few steps he took. In the fear of a
fatigue which might prevent his reaching his
object, he dared not over-exert himself, but
he walked as fast as he thought wise. He
rested himself now and again by breaking

into a jog-trot whenever the incline of the ground was not too abrupt. He had covered nearly two-thirds of the distance from the brow of the hill to where he might hope to find the bridge when he caught the first glimpse of his pursuers; the outline of a single man stood out against the horizon. He quickened his pace.

When next he looked back there were four or five men gathered together in a little group about the tall chief. As his eyes were on them the chief waved one hand, and the warriors sprang forward in a brisk run. He had seen them, and he knew that they could see him. It was now a question of speed. If he could get across the bridge safe and sound, it might be that he could hold it until nightfall should give him an-other chance of escape. If they should catch up to him on the open ground, or if there should not be any bridge at the spot where he hoped to find it, then all would be over; his life would not be worth an hour's purchase, however dearly he might sell it.

The ground favored him just then, and he dropped into a gentle run. Soon the declivity became too steep for so rapid a progress, and he fell back to a walk. Again he looked at his pursuers. The little group about the chief, not so compact now as when he had first seen it, had covered more than a quarter of the distance which had separated them. And behind these were three other groups rushing towards him, stretching across the slope one after the other.

Mr. Stead set his teeth and strode forward. For five minutes he toiled steadily upward, as he neared his goal the ascent was steeper. When he could no longer resist the desire to see whether or not his enemies were gaining on him, he turned his head again. The chief and his followers were but a few hundred feet behind him— scarcely beyond bow-shot, and tailing out over the inclined plain were half a hundred more White Indians, all racing towards him. As they saw him looking at them they raised fierce yells of hatred.

In ten yards more Mr. Stead came out on the brink of the river, which rolled along in a deep gulf below, whence it sent out a cloud of spray from a thundering cataract. Scarce a hundred feet before him the gulf was spanned by a slight swinging bridge.

Mr. Stead saw it, and he gave a gasp of relief ; knowing there was now no more need to husband his strength, he rushed forward as fast as he could. When he came to the foot-path which led to the bridge he was still a hundred feet in advance of the nearest of his pursuers. He crossed the frail and vibrating structure as swiftly as he dared, though it trembled beneath his tread. and swung from side to side until it almost threw him off into the dark abyss below, where the river raged fiercely along. As he was toiling up the farther half of the bridge the White Indians arrived on the brink of the cliff behind him. They paused, and two of them fitted arrows to their bows. One of these missiles missed Mr. Stead, the other struck him in the back of the waist, and broke off against the plates of gold which protected his person at that place.

When he set foot on the firm land and faced about, three of his foes were already on the bridge and crossing over. He stood

8

still in the centre of the path and took deliberate aim and fired. The foremost Indian threw up his hands and fell sideways from the bridge. A second shot struck the next man in the right thigh, and he dropped back, vainly grasping, as he turned in the air, at the ropes which supported the fragile pathway, and dropped down into the dark water which was roaring along the bottom of the chasm more than a hundred feet below. The third man had but just started on his perilous passage : when his two predecessors perished so suddenly, he hesitated for a second, then he sprang forward again. The chief stretched out his arm and stayed the other White Indians as they came up, waiting to see what might be the fate of the third man. Mr. Stead held his fire until this man — a tall, handsome fellow — was within fifty feet of him, then he pulled the trigger, and the pursuer, shot through the heart, sprang up into the air, and fell down into the gulf below, knotted into a convulsive ball. Then Mr. Stead, seeing that there was no movement on the part of his enemies to attack again, reloaded his revolver.

By this time nearly all the warriors had assembled on the other side. Several of the late comers were about to run forward on the bridge, but the tall chief called them back. Suddenly a flight of arrows shot across the chasm, and fluttered down before Mr. Stead's feet. He was just out of range. But he thought it best to discourage any desire they might have to use him as a mark : taking careful aim, he fired his revolver again, and the bullet broke the chief's arm. An awful yell arose at this, and for the third time the chief had to restrain the impetuosity of his followers. Mr. Stead could not but admire the reckless bravery of his foes, eager to sacrifice their lives to avenge their leader.

For a few minutes there was a respite. While an old man carefully bandaged the chief's wounded arm, the others gathered about them and raised a weird, irregular, pathetic chant, which seemed part of the ceremonial of cure. Mr. Stead took advantage of the lull to consider the situation. So long as he could hold the end of the bridge he was safe ; they could advance

across it only one at a time, and their numbers were therefore of no advantage to them.
Yet this security was but temporary; he
dared not abandon his post, for his safety
depended on his defending it. He was
forced to remain where he was, and to make
no attempt to proceed on his journey. His
foes outnumbered him fifty to one. They
could tire him out, and they could starve
him out, if they were willing to settle down
to a siege. They might even separate, and
while one detachment kept him at bay, the
other might retrace its steps to the place
where he shot the bird of ill omen, and
where their canoes were; then, crossing the
river in these, they might come down and
take him in the rear.

This scheme seemed to have occurred to
the chief at the very moment that it suggested itself to Mr. Stead. From his com-
manding position the American saw the
leader of the White Indians call a man forward and give him a series of orders, accompanied by gestures which Mr. Stead
found no difficulty in interpreting. When
he had received his instructions the chosen

leader of the detachment went among his
comrades and picked out a dozen of them.
These he drew up in line before the chief,
who spoke a few words of advice, apparently, and of warning. When the chief ceased,
his followers raised a shout of anticipatory
triumph, shaking their weapons in the air,
and casting looks of hatred against the
single American. Then the designated
group broke away from the main body and
ran back on their own trail. In less than
five minutes they were lost to sight.

Mr. Stead had no doubt as to the meaning of the departure of this detachment of
his foes. He knew that in a definite time
— probably four or five hours — he would
be outflanked. With an enemy behind him,
against whom he could have no protection,
his doom would soon be sealed. He saw
that if he wished to save his life, and to
bear off the treasure which had been con-
fided to him, and which he had bound himself to convey safely to its destination,
he must do something, and he must do it
quickly.

His first thought was to pick off his opponents one by one, as he had wounded the chief. But a moment's reflection showed the impossibility of this proceeding. There were still nearly two-score White Indians at the other end of the bridge. By taking them unawares, he might hope to kill ten or a dozen. But what would this profit him? The rest would hide themselves behind the rocks, and, securely under cover, they could then bide their time, exposing themselves only when their comrades might announce their arrival on his side of the river. And yet another reason deterred him. His stock of ammunition was limited; he had barely a score more cartridges.

To remain where he was would be impossible, and to retreat while his foes might at once cross the bridge after him was to invite an immediate death. His only hope of safety was so to bar their passage across the river that he might continue his journey without fear of their following him.

The bridge was of a kind uncommon in Guiana, but frequent enough in the passes of the Andes, where it was found when the soldiers of Pizarro first trod the soil of Peru.

It is probably the most primitive form of the suspension-bridge. It consists of two stout cables stretched across the valley in a pendent arc. These cables are made of the pliant woody stems of climbing plants, twisted into bush-ropes, as they are called; and they are almost unbreakable by any strain likely to be put on them. These tough and flexible cables are fastened to huge rocks on each side of the gulf, running parallel with each other, less than a yard apart. They are floored with light planks laid across from cable to cable, and securely lashed by bands of mamurie, a finer cord made of osier withes or lianas. On each side of the main cables and a little above them is another slighter bush-rope, intended to serve as a hand-rail for those who trust themselves on the fragile and oscillating bridge.

To block a delicate suspension - bridge like this so as to debar a passage across it would be impossible. But as Mr. Stead, under the pressure of impending death, took stock of the situation and considered the matter in every light, he saw that it might not be impossible to destroy the bridge. Tough as were the huge cables of twisted vines, he believed that he could saw through them with the knife which every South-American traveller must needs carry. Unfortunately, as he found, he could not do the work of destruction except in full sight of the beleaguering foe. On his side of the river a lip of rock thrusting well out into the valley had been chosen as the landing-place; the two cables had been stretched tightly across, then they disappeared into the earth, being apparently made fast to subterranean stones.

Mr. Stead made a most careful examination. His one chance of safety was to destroy the bridge, and the one place where this could best be done was at the very verge of the precipice from which it projected. In fact, to work to advantage, Mr. Stead saw that he would have to bend forward over the yawning chasm. For this reason he removed his treasure - belt or jacket, laying it at his feet. He looked to his revolver, preparing a little pile of cartridges ready to his hand, wisely thinking that the White Indians would probably renew their attack as soon as they discovered what he was doing. He sharpened his knife. Then he seated himself between the two cables at the edge of the shelf of rock, and began the task of cutting them in two.

He had labored for several minutes before the White Indians took any notice of his movements. Then one of them began to watch him suspiciously, and called the attention of the chief. In a minute they discovered what his object was. A wild shriek of rage arose, and two men seized their weapons and sprang forward along the bridge. Mr. Stead shifted his knife to his left hand and grasped his revolver. The two White Indians came on as fast as their swinging foothold would allow. When they were within forty feet of him he fired, and the first man fell back. He fired again, and the second man, tripping on his comrade's body, which lay dead across the footpath, dropped down, turning spasmodically until he struck the water below, and was hurried out of sight.

Mr. Stead reloaded his revolver and resumed work.

Other White Indians hung back just at the entrance to the bridge, doubting and undecided. The American kept his eye on them while he went on with his labors. The vegetable fibre of the bush-rope was singularly resisting, and to cut it called for strength and skill and time. There was a hesitation among his adversaries which gave him opportunity almost to sever the cable at his right hand; at least it was more than half cut through, when his knife broke, and the best part of the blade slipped into the abyss.

At this moment he noticed an unusual movement among the White Indians. They had withdrawn a little to a clear space on one side, and there they had formed a ring around the chief. Chanting a wild but simple refrain, they circled about their wounded leader, who stood erect in the centre, beating time by striking the ground with a hollow bamboo staff he held in his unwounded hand. The rude and monotonous song they sang resembled a dirge, wailing and funereal; it was broken at regular intervals by discordant shouts.

With the stump of his knife still serviceable, Mr. Stead was at work on the cable at his left; but he never took his eyes from the enemy. He could not guess their purpose, but he felt sure that it portended evil to him, and that he must be more than ever on his guard.

Suddenly there was a shout louder than the rest, and one of the White Indians broke from the ring and stood on one side. Then the same monotonous wailing began again; and in due season there was another loud shout, and a second man left the ring, and took his place by the side of the first. A third time the rude chanting began, the chief beating on the ground with his bamboo staff, and after the same interval there was again a loud shout, and a third man took position with the other two.

This proceeding puzzled Mr. Stead, and, without slacking his labor on the left-hand cable, he bent his attention to the doings of his foes. Strange as was the rough chant, which soon began again for the fourth time, there seemed to the American something familiar in its rhythm. He had no memory of having ever heard it before, yet it rang with a pulsation vaguely resembling something that had fallen on his ears somewhere. For a while he could not place it. But as it concluded for the fourth time with a shout, and a fourth man stood aside, there came back to Mr. Stead the echo of a foolish rhyme of his childhood, a jingle of gibberish, unmeaning, but useful, for it served to designate that one of his boyish playfellows whose duty it should be to chase and touch the rest of them.

Then, as the strange strain arose for the fifth time, the American knew what it was, and he saw its significance. It was a counting-out rhyme, by which the followers of the tall chief were choosing men for a special purpose. Different as was the doggerel he had used in his boyhood from that which he heard now, there was the same marked regularity of beat, the same simple rhythm, and, above all, the same result.

A fifth man took his position beside the others who had thus been chosen by chance.

When the song ceased again, a sixth man stepped out of the ring and joined his five comrades.

Mr. Stead was working away steadily, and he had made a deep cut in the cable at his left, softer and more rotten than that on his right, so that his labor was not harder, though he now had but the stump of a knife.

After the six men had been selected the rhythmic chant ceased, and the ring was abandoned. The White Indians gathered about the chief to receive his instructions.

Then, and then only, did Mr. Stead discover their intent. The chief knew that the revolver could fire only six shots without reloading. He had picked out six men to sacrifice themselves by drawing these six shots, after which the American would be defenceless. The rest would rush forward. The plan was simple, and it bid fair to succeed.

Mr. Stead worked on with desperate energy. Every second was precious to him. If they would delay their attack but five minutes longer, the bridge would be cut, and he would be secure from pursuit.

But they did not delay a single minute. The six men stepped to the head of the bridge, and stood one behind the other, ready to advance. The chief came forward beside them and raised his hand. They fell on their knees, and he waved his staff above their heads, while the rest of the White Indians uttered a shrill cry, half defiant and half sorrowful. Then they arose and girded themselves for the certain death to which they were going. The others fell in line behind them, headed by the chief.

Mr. Stead saw that the moment had come. He rose to his feet to await the attack.

A moment more and it came. The chief gave the signal. A yell of rage and hate broke from the throats of the White Indians, and the six doomed men set forward to cross the bridge, in single file, followed by the chief and the rest of their fellow-tribesmen. More accustomed to the oscillations of so frail a structure, their progress was far more rapid than Mr. Stead's was when he had been forced to run across the bridge with the enemy close behind him.

When the first of the six had reached the

body of the man who had been killed when Mr. Stead began to cut the cable, the American fired, and the White Indian plunged forward head-first into the chasm. Then Mr. Stead fired again, and the second man, reeling forward, grasped the corpse which lay across the bridge, and together the two —the dead and the dying—dropped headlong into the gulf below. A third shot, and a fourth shot, and a fifth shot, and three more of the assailants were swept from the bridge.

At the sixth shot the revolver missed fire, and the last of the chosen six was within twenty feet of Mr. Stead when, on the second attempt, the trigger did its duty, and the bullet found its billet in the doomed man's heart.

The six shots had done their work, and the six men had done theirs. The seventh man—the chief himself—was not more than twenty-five feet distant when the last ball left the American's revolver. There was no time to load again. The best Mr. Stead could do was to fight for his life man to man, at the head of the bridge. He grasped

his revolver by the barrel, and he stooped
and with his left hand seized the stump of
the knife. He thought that the seconds he
had yet to live were counted, but he did not
blanch; he looked death in the face and
flinched not.

But it was not to be. Fortune favors the
brave. Though he had not had time to cut
the cables wholly in two, he had weakened
them so that they were unable to bear the
strain of the whole band of White Indians.
The foremost was barely a yard from the
end of the bridge when the left cable parted, and Mr. Stead saw his foes fall together
into the dark river below. With a mighty
effort the chief, who was at the head of the
line, reached forward to clutch the solid
earth. His hand grasped the treasure-belt,
which had lain at Mr. Stead's feet all through
the fight, and it clasped this with the grip of
desperation. In the sudden emotion of de-
liverance from death, Mr. Stead was not
prompt enough to see this minor danger,
and the chief of the White Indians bore
with him to the bottom of the turbulent
river the gold which the American had

"THE CABLE PARTED, AND HIS FOES FELL
INTO THE RIVER BELOW"

risked his life to save. To expect ever to recover it is hopeless.

There is no need to delay your readers with a detailed account of Mr. Stead's return to civilization. As soon as he was free from the danger of pursuit, he set out for the village of friendly Indians, which he found, as he had expected, some fifteen miles farther down the river. Here he was well received, and supplied with the means of continuing his journey.

While at this village he made inquiry for Austin, who had basely deserted him in his hour of peril. To Mr. Stead's great grief—although not at all to his surprise—he found that nothing had been heard of Austin. And as yet nothing has been heard of the fellow. It was nightfall when Austin thrust loose from the bank and started alone on his voyage down the river. In his fright it is probable that he forgot the rapids before him until -it was too late to turn back, or even to check his canoe. Barely a mile be· low the point where he abandoned Mr. Stead, the river becomes narrow and the banks precipitous, and there is a succession of cata-

9

racts. It was above this gulch that Mr.
Stead fought for his life, and it was probably in this gulch that Austin met his death
by the wrecking of his canoe in the turmoil
of waters. If once the wood-skin had got
caught in the rush of the rapids, there would
be no possible chance of escape for its solitary occupant. That this is what happened
to Austin seems now beyond doubt, since
no other explanation of his disappearance is possible. Coward as the fellow
was, it is sad to think of his dark and
lonely voyage to a certain and horrible
death.

It was only the night before last that Mr.
Stead arrived here at Georgetown. Yesterday I had the pleasure of meeting him, and
of hearing the full tale of his adventures
from his own lips. In transcribing these for
your readers I have passed the night. It
seems to me to be a duty which a man of
letters owes his fellow-man to set forth simply and succinctly so brave a fight against
terrible odds as that which Mr. Stead has
just fought. It is the study of a strong
character like his, and of brave deeds like

this, which restores our faith in our common humanity.

I have thought it best also that the facts of this outrage on an American citizen should be laid before the people of the United States as soon as possible, that the State Department might be moved to take prompt action.

This letter goes back to you by favor of Mr. Joshua Hoffman, whose beautiful steam-yacht, the *Rhadamanthus*, is to sail for New York this afternoon. Mr. Hoffman has been spending a fortnight in these waters; he expresses himself as delighted with the scenery, and much benefited in health by the rest he has obtained.

I expect to sail for the Orinoco early next week, and you shall hear from me again at the very first opportunity.　　　　A. Z.

II.

FROM THE "GOTHAM GAZETTE" OF APRIL 22.

OFFICE OF THE ESSEQUIBO GOLD COMPANY,
76 BROADWAY, NEW YORK, *April* 21.

TO THE EDITOR OF THE *Gotham Gazette:*

SIR,—I have read with interest the entertaining letter from an Occasional Correspondent which you have published this morning, and which purports to give an account of an extraordinary outrage recently committed in British Guiana on an American named Stead by a tribe of hitherto unknown White Indians. I hate to have to spoil so sensational a story, but I see that there is a sort of to-be-continued-in-our-next at the end of his letter, and I feel, therefore, that I am only anticipating the correction the Occasional Correspondent will be forced to make as soon as he knows what has happened since he wrote. Perhaps you will excuse me if I suggest that before writing he might have inquired more carefully as to the value of the information he received.

What has happened since then is that the man Stead was arrested yesterday for theft and for attempted murder. The thing he tried to steal was the gold intrusted to him to convey from the mines to the coast. The man he tried to murder was his accomplice in the intended theft—Austin.

When I inform you that Austin is in New York, that he has confessed fully his share in the robbery, and that he has accused Stead of an attempt to put him out of the way, it may occur to some of those who may have read the exciting letter of the Occasional Correspondent that he is a gentleman of an unduly confiding nature, and that he has inadvertently allowed himself to be used by a rascal.

The exact facts of the matter are that Stead and Austin, being intrusted with the gold of the Essequibo Gold Company, conspired to steal it. When they had arrived near the cañon across which Stead claims to have fought so brave a fight against such long odds, they dug a hole and buried the gold, Stead telling Austin that he would invent a tale of an attack by the White Indians, who exist in local superstition, but whom nobody has ever seen. That night the thieves fell out, and Stead set Austin adrift in the canoe without a paddle, knowing that there was a water-fall ahead, and hoping that his accomplice would be drowned. Apparently Austin is reserved for another fate; his canoe sank on a rock in shallow water; he waded ashore, and was taken up by a band of friendly Indians, with whom he journeyed slowly to the coast. He arrived at Georgetown about midnight, a few hours before the *Rhadamanthus* sailed. Going to a friend's house, he heard the story Stead had been telling, and in fear of his life he determined to fly the country. This friend had done some trifling service for Mr. Joshua Hoffman, and thus Austin succeeded in being taken aboard the *Rhadamanthus* without the knowledge of the people of Georgetown. There is a pleasant irony in the fact that the very yacht which bore away the Occasional Correspondent's account of Stead's single-handed combat with impossible White Indians over a non-existent bridge should convey also the one man who knew the whole truth.

On his arrival here yesterday Austin came down to the office of the Essequibo Gold Company and surrendered himself. He made a clean breast of his share in the attempt to rob the company. We cabled at once to the Georgetown police. We learned that Stead had been away in the interior for a week, and that he had just returned. He was about to take ship for England when he was arrested. The stolen gold was found in his possession.

I have to apologize for this trespass on your space, but enemies of the Essequibo Gold Company try to use ghost stories like that of the Occasional Correspondent to depress the securities of the company, and as its president it is my duty to prevent this. Besides, just now I am a bull on the market.

Your obedient servant,

SAMUEL SARGENT.

(1888.)

THE NEW MEMBER OF THE CLUB

THE NEW MEMBER OF THE CLUB

I.

THE FIRST SATURDAY.

SOMETHING must have detained me that evening, since it was nearly midnight when I arrived at the club, and I hate to be so tardy as that, for some of our best members are married men now, who never stay out after one o'clock, or two at the very furthest. Besides, the supper is served at eleven, and the first comers take all the pleasant little tables which line the walls of the grill-room, leaving for the belated arrivals only the large table which runs down the middle of the room.

As every one knows, ours is a club whose members mainly belong to the allied arts. Of course, now and then a millionaire manages to get elected by passing himself off as an art-patron; but for the most part, the men one meets there are authors, actors, architects, and artists on canvas or in marble. So it is that the supper served at eleven every Saturday night, from October to May, is the occasion of many a pleasant meeting with friends who happen in quite informally. When the week's work is done, it is good to have a place to forgather with one's fellows—a place where one can eat, and drink, and smoke, a place where one can sit in a cosey corner, and talk shop, and swap stories.

I cannot now recall the reason why I was late on the evening in question, nor just what evening it was, although I am sure that it was after Founder's Night (which is New-year's Eve), and before Ladies' Day (which is Shakespeare's birthday). I remember only that it was nearly midnight, and that as I entered the reading-room I was hailed by Astroyd, the actor.

"I say, Arthur," he cried, "you are the very man we want to take the third seat at our table. You must have a bird and a bottle with me to-night, for this is the last evening I shall have at the club for many a long day."

"Are you going on the road again?" I asked, with interest; for I liked Astroyd, and I knew we should all regret his departure.

" I'm off for Australia, that's where I'm going," he answered; "thirty per cent. of the gross, with five hundred a week guaranteed. I take the vestibule limited at ten in the morning, and I'm not half packed yet. So we must get over supper at once. Besides, I want you to meet a friend of mine."

Then, for the first time, I noticed the gentleman who was standing by the side of Astroyd, a little behind him. The actor stepped back and introduced us :—

"Mr. Harrington Cockshaw, Mr. Arthur Penn."

As we shook hands, Astroyd added, "Cockshaw is a new member of the club."

At that moment one of the waiters came up to tell the actor that the table he had asked for was vacant at last, whereupon we all three went into the grill-room, and sat down to our supper at once. I had just time to note that Mr. Cockshaw was an insignificant little man with a bristling, sandy mustache. When he took his place opposite to me I saw that he had light-brown eyes, and that his expression suggested a strange admixture of shyness and self-assertion.

While the waiter was drawing the cork, Mr. Cockshaw bent forward, and said, with the merest hint of condescension in his manner, "I'm delighted to meet you this evening, Mr. Penn, partly because just this very afternoon I have been reading your admirable essay 'On the Sonnet and its History.'"

I was about to murmur my appreciation of this complimentary coincidence when Astroyd broke in.

"Arthur knows a sonnet when he sees it," he said, "and he can turn off as good a topical song as any man in New York."

"I can't write, myself," Mr. Cockshaw went on; "I wish I could—though I don't suppose anybody would read it if I did. But my brother-in-law is connected with

"WE WENT INTO THE GRILL-ROOM, AND SAT DOWN TO SUPPER"

literature, in a way; he's a publisher; he's the Co. of Carpenter & Co."

Just then Astroyd caught sight of Harry Brackett standing in the broad doorway.

" Here you are, Harry," he cried; " join us. Have a stirrup-cup with me. I haven't seen you for moons—not for 'steen moons —and I'm off for Australia to-morrow by the bright light."

"Isn't America good enough for you?" asked Harry Brackett, as he lounged over to us.

" Not at the beginning of next season, it isn't," the actor declared. " Electing a President of these United States is more fun than a farce-comedy, and for two weeks before the Tuesday following the first Monday in November you can't club people into the theatre."

"That's so, sometimes," responded Harry, as Astroyd and I made room for him at our little table; " and I don't see how we are going to keep up public interest in Gettysburg next fall, unless there's an old-time bloody-shirt campaign. If there is, I'll get a phonograph, and agree to let every visitor to the panorama sample a genuine Rebel yell."

Astroyd caught the expression of perplexity that flitted across the face of the new member of the club, so he made haste to introduce the new-comer.

"Mr. Brackett, Mr. Cockshaw," he said; adding as they bowed, "Mr. Brackett is now the manager of the panorama of the Battle of Gettysburg."

"And I'm going to be buried on the field of battle," Harry Brackett interjected, "if I can't scare up some new way to boom the thing soon."

"I should not think that so fine a work of art would need any booming," Mr. Cockshaw smilingly remarked. "I had the pleasure of going in to see it again only yesterday. It is a great painting, extraordinarily vivid, exactly like the real thing—at least so I am told. I was not at the battle myself, but my brother-in-law commanded a North Carolina brigade in Pickett's charge; he lost a leg there."

"I don't know but what a one-legged Confederate might draw," Harry Brackett soliloquized. "The lecturer we have now is no good: he gives his celebrated imita-

tion of a wounded soldier drinking out of a
canteen so often and so realistically that
he is always on the diminuendo of a jag—
when he isn't on the crescendo."

" If he gets loaded," said Astroyd, promptly, "why don't you fire him ?"

" It's all very well for you to make jokes,"
Harry Brackett returned, "but it isn't easy
to get a lecturer who really looks like an
old soldier. Besides, his name is worth
something; it is so short that we can print
it in big letters on a single line—Colonel
Mark Day. I shouldn't wonder if he had
the two shortest names in all the United
States."

"It *is* a short name," said the little man,
as though pleased to get into conversation
again. "It is a very short name, indeed.
But I know a shorter. My brother-in-law
has one letter less in his, and one syllable
more. His name is Eli Low."

Harry Brackett looked at the new member of the club for a moment as though he
were going to make a pertinent reply. Then
apparently he thought better of it, and said
nothing.

10

As the conversation flagged I asked Astroyd if he was going to act in San Francisco on his way to Australia.

"No," he answered; "I go straight through
without stopping, but I've got two weeks at
'Frisco coming home, and I shall play my
way back over the Northern Pacific. You
know Duluth and Superior are both three-
night stands now."

"San Francisco is falling off every year,"
Harry Brackett commented. "The flush
times are all over on the coast. I remember the days when a big attraction could
play to ten thousand dollars three weeks
running."

"Yes," Astroyd assented; "'Frisco is not
the show-town it used to be, though we took
nineteen thousand three hundred and forty
in two weeks, last time I was there."

"Perhaps somebody will strike another
bonanza before you get back," I suggested;
"and if there is another boom you can do a
big business."

"I came near going out to the Pacific
coast last summer," said Mr. Cockshaw, "to
look after a chicken-ranch I'm interested in

near Monotony Dam. Somehow I couldn't find time to get away, so I had to give it up. But my brother-in-law was an old Forty-niner, and he told me he once found a seven-pound nugget in a pocket. He had a claim at a camp called Hell-to-pay."

" I've played there in the old days," Astroyd remarked, promptly. "We did ' Hamlet ' on a stage made of two billiard-tables shoved back to the end of the biggest saloon in the camp. But the place experienced a change of heart long ago ; it has three churches now, and calls itself Eltopia to-day."

" It was a pretty tough town in my brother-in-law's time," the little man declared. "He told me he had often seen two and three men shot in a morning."

I had noticed that when Mr. Cockshaw mentioned the strange luck of his brother-in-law's finding an extraordinary nugget in a pocket, Harry Brackett had looked up and fixed his eyes on the face of the little man as though to spy out a contradiction between Mr. Cockshaw's expression and his conversation. So when our little party

broke up, and Astroyd had said farewell
and departed, taking Cockshaw with him,
I was not at all surprised to have the manager of the panorama stop me as I was making ready to go home.

"I say, Arthur," he began, "who is that
little fellow, anyhow—the one with the alleged brother-in-law?"

I answered that I had never met Mr.
Cockshaw until that evening, and that Astroyd had declared him to be a new member
of the club.

"Then that's why I haven't seen him before," Harry Brackett responded. "Queer
little cuss, isn't he? Somehow he looked
as though he might be a dealer in misfit
coffins, or something of that sort. And the
way he kept blowing about that brother-in-
law of his would make a stuffed bird laugh.
I wonder what his business really is. What's
more, I wonder who he is."

To satisfy this curiosity of Harry's we
asked a dozen different men if they knew
anything about a new member of the club
named Cockshaw, and we found that nobody had ever heard of him. Apparently

Astroyd had been the only man there he had ever seen before that evening.

Harry Brackett finally sent for the proposal book, to see who had been his sponsors. He found that J. Harrington Cockshaw, Retired, had been proposed by Mr. Joshua Hoffman, the millionaire philanthropist, and that he had been seconded by John Abram Carkendale, the second vice-president of the Methuselah Life Insurance Company. But we could not ask them about him, because old Mr. Hoffman was on his steam-yacht *Rhadamanthus* in the Mediterranean, somewhere between Gibraltar and Cairo; and Mr. Carkendale was out west, somewhere between Denver and Salt Lake City, on his semi-annual tour of inspection of the agencies of the Methuselah Life. And Astroyd, who had introduced him to us, and who might fairly be presumed to be able to give us some information concerning the new member, was about to start for Australia.

" So all we know about him," said Harry Brackett, summing up the result of our researches, "is that his name is J. Harrington

Cockshaw, that he is Retired — whatever that may mean — that he knows Joshua Hoffman and John Abram Carkendale well enough to have them propose him here, and that he has a brother-in-law, whose name is Eli Low, who was in California in '49, who lost a leg at Gettysburg in Pickett's charge, and who is now a partner in the publishing house of Carpenter & Co."

And with that information Harry Brackett had then perforce to be content.

II.

THE SECOND SATURDAY.

The next Saturday evening I arrived at the club a little earlier. I had been dining with Delancey Jones, the architect, and we played piquet at his house for a couple of hours after dinner. When we entered the club together it was scarcely half-past ten; and yet we found half a dozen regular Saturday night attendants already gathered together in the main hall just beside the huge fireplace emblazoned with the motto of the club. Starrington, the tragedian, was one of the group, and Judge Gillespie was another; Rupert de Ruyter, the novelist, was a third, and John Sharp, the young African explorer, was a fourth; while Harry Brackett sat back on a broad sofa by the side of Mr. Harrington Cockshaw, the new member of the club.

When we joined the party the judge was describing the methods and the machinery of a gang of safe-breakers whom he had recently sent to Sing Sing for a bank burglary.

"The bank almost deserved to be robbed," the judge concluded, "because it had not availed itself of the latest improvements in safe-building."

"When a bank gets a chilled-iron safe, it's a cold day for the burglar, I suppose," said Rupert de Ruyter, who occasionally condescended to a trifling jest of this sort.

"A chilled-iron safe is better than a wooden desk, of course," Harry Brackett remarked; "but the safe-breakers keep almost even with the safe-makers. With a kit of the latest tools a burglar can get into pretty nearly anything—except the kingdom of Heaven."

"And it is almost as hard to get a really fire-proof safe as it is to get one burglar-proof," said Jones. "The building I put up for a fire-insurance company out in New-ark two years ago burned down before the carpenters were out of it, although the company had moved into its own office on the first floor, and about half of the books in the safe were charred into uselessness, like the manuscripts of Herculaneum."

"I was never burned out, myself," Mr. Cockshaw declared, taking advantage of a lull in the conversation, "but my brother-in-law was president of a lumber company in Chicago at the time of the great fire; and he told me that most of the books of the firm were destroyed, but that wherever there had been any writing in pencil this was legi-ble, even though the paper itself was burned to a crisp, while the writing in ink had been usually obliterated by the heat."

The hint of self-assertion which might have been detected in Mr. Cockshaw's

manner a week before had now totally disappeared, as though he felt himself quite
at home in the club already, and had no
need to defend his position. His manner
was wholly unobtrusive and almost depre-
catory. There was even a certain vague
hesitancy of speech which I had not noticed when we had met before. His voice
was smooth, as though to match his smooth
face, clean-shaven except for the faint little
mustache which bristled above the full lips.

So soft-spoken had he been that only
Harry Brackett and I had heard this contribution of his to the conversation; and
under the lead of Judge Gillespie the talk
turned off from the ways of burglars to the
treatment of criminals, and thus to the
rights and wrongs of prisoners. Something
that Rupert de Ruyter said started off John
Sharp—usually taciturn and disinclined to
talk—and he began by denouncing the evils
of the slave-hunting raids the Arabs make
in Africa. To show us just how hideous,
how vile, how inhuman a thing slavery is,
he was led to describe to us one of his own
experiences in the heart of the dark conti-

nent, and to tell us how he had followed for days on the heels of a slave-caravan, finding it easy to keep the trail because of the half-dozen or more corpses he passed every day —corpses of slaves, women and men, who fell out of the ranks from weakness, and who either had been killed outright or else allowed to die of starvation.

We all listened with intense interest as John Sharp told us what he had seen, for it was a rare thing for him to speak about his African experiences; sometimes I had wondered whether they were not too painful for him willingly to recall them.

"I wish I could go to Africa," said Rupert de Ruyter. "I know that it is a land of battle, murder, and sudden death, but I believe that a picture of the life there under the equator, a faithful presentment of existence as it is, as direct and as simple as one could make it—I believe a story of that sort might easily make as big a hit as *Uncle Tom's Cabin.*

"And it might do as much good," said the judge. "There is no hope for Africa till the slave-trade is rooted out absolutely.

Until that is done once for all, this sending out of missionaries is a mere waste of
money."

"Yet the missionaries at least set an example of courage and self-sacrifice," suggested Mr. Cockshaw, timidly. "Of course
I don't know anything about the matter per-
sonally, but my brother-in-law was with Stanley on that search for Livingstone, and I am
merely repeating what I have heard him say
often."

After the new member of the club had
said this, I became conscious immediately
that Harry Brackett was gazing at me intently. At last I looked up, and when he
caught my eye he winked. I glanced away
at once, but I was at no loss to interpret
the meaning of this signal.

For a while the talk rambled along un-
eventfully, and then some one suddenly
suggested supper. Ten minutes thereafter
our little gathering was dissolved. Judge
Gillespie and John Sharp had gone up into
the library to consult a new map of Africa.
Starrington and de Ruyter had secured a
little table in the grill-room, and pending

the arrival of the ingredients for the Welsh rabbits (for the making of which the novelist was famous), they were deep in a discussion of the play which the actor wished to have written for him.   Mr. Cockshaw, Harry Brackett, Delancey Jones, and I had made ourselves comfortable at a round table in the bow - window of the grillroom.

Perhaps it was the pewter mugs depending from the hooks below the shelf which ran all around the room at the top of the wainscot which suggested to Harry Brackett mugs of another kind, for he suddenly turned on Jones abruptly.

"And how are the twins?" he asked.

"The twins are all right," Jones answered, "and so am I, thank you."

"And how old are they now?" Harry Brackett inquired further.

"Two months," the happy parent responded.

"To think of you with a pair of twins," mused the manager of the panorama.   "I believe you said there was a pair of them?"

"I suppose I did suggest that number

when I revealed the fact that my family had been increased by twins."

"Well, I never thought it of you, I confess," Harry Brackett continued. "You are an architect by profession, a lover of the picturesque, an admirer of all that is beautiful in an odd and unexpected way; and so I never dreamed that you would do anything so commonplace as to have two babies just alike, and of just the same size, and the same age."

"It is queer, I admit," Jones retorted; "but then this is leap-year, you know, and there are always more twins born in leap-year than in any other year."

"I never heard that before," Harry Brackett declared. "I wonder why it is?"

"Perhaps," said the architect, as he took down his own pewter mug, "it is simply because leap-year is one day longer than any other year."

"Oh!" ejaculated the man who had let himself into this trap; then he rang a bell on the table, and told the waiter who came in response to take Mr. Jones's order.

"I wonder whether the prevalence of

twins has anything to do with the periodicity of the spots on the sun," I suggested. "Almost every other phenomenon has been ascribed to this cause."

"I believe that the statistics of twins have never been properly investigated," remarked Mr. Cockshaw, gently. "I have not studied the subject myself, but my brother-in-law was a pupil of Spitzer's in Vienna, and he was much interested in the matter. He was preparing a paper in which he set forth a theory of his own, and he was going to read it at the Medical Conference in Vienna during the Exhibition of 1873, but unfortunately he died ten days before the conference met."

"Who died?" Harry Brackett asked with startling directness—"Spitzer or your brother-in-law?"

"Dr. Spitzer is alive still," the new member answered; "it was my brother-in-law who died."

"I'm glad of that," said Harry Brackett to me, scarcely lowering his voice, although apparently Mr. Cockshaw did not hear him. "If he's dead and buried, perhaps we sha'n't hear anything more about him."

And it was a fact that although we four, Jones and I, Cockshaw and Harry Brackett, sat at that little table in the grill-room for perhaps two hours longer, and then went back into the hall for another smoke, we did not hear the new member of the club refer again that night to his brother-in-law.

III.

THE THIRD SATURDAY.

A week later I was sitting in my study, trying to polish into lilting smoothness a tale in verse which I had written for the Christmas number of *The Metropolis;* and in my labors on this lyric legend I had quite forgotten that it was Saturday night. I had just laid down my pen with the con-viction that whether the poem was good or bad, it was, at least, the best I could do, when Harry Brackett broke in on me, and insisted on bearing me off to the club.

"I want you to be there to-night," he asserted, " for a particular reason."

But what this particular reason might be he refused to declare. I ventured on a guess at it, when we were on our way to the club wrapped in our rain-coats, and trusting to a single umbrella to shield us both from the first spring-squall.

"I lunched at the club to-day," he said casually, just after a sudden gust of wind had turned our umbrella inside out, "and I heard that man Cockshaw telling Laurence Laughton that he had never seen a great race himself, but that his brother-in-law had been in Louisville when Tenbroeck beat Molly Macarthy."

"That's why you are haling me to the club through this storm," I cried. "You want a companion to help you listen to Mr. Cockshaw's statements."

"I want you to be there to-night," he answered. "And you will soon see why last Saturday, when I heard that that brother-in-law of Cockshaw's was dead, I gave a sigh of relief. I thought we were quit of him for good and all. But we are not.

It was not Wednesday before Cockshaw
had resurrected the corpse, and galvanized
it into spasmodic existence. Every night
this week he has been dining at the club."

"The brother-in-law?" I asked.

"No," he replied, "only Cockshaw. If I
could see the brother-in-law there in the
flesh, I'd pay for his dinner with pleasure.
But that's a sight I can never hope to behold. The man has had too many strange
experiences to survive. Why, do you know
—but there, I can't tell you half the things
Cockshaw has told us now and again during
the past week. All I can say is that he has
literally exuded miscellaneous misinforma-
tion about that alleged brother-in-law of his.
No more remarkable man ever lived since
the Admirable Crichton—and I never heard
that *he* had nine lives like a cat."

I deprecated Harry Brackett's heat in
speaking of Cockshaw, and I told him that
I thought the new member of the club was
a most modest and unassuming little man.

"That's just what is so annoying," returned my companion. "If he put on
frills, and lied about himself and his own

11

surprising adventures, I could forgive him; but there it is — the little semicolon of a cuss never boasts about his own deeds; he just caps all our stories with some wild, weird tale of his brother-in-law's doings. It is the meanest trick out. Do you believe he ever had a brother-in-law?"

This query was propounded as we stood before the door of the club.

"Why shouldn't I?" was my answer.

"Oh, you carry credulity to an extreme," Harry Brackett responded as he shut his umbrella. "Now I don't. I don't believe this man Cockshaw ever had a brother-in-law, alive or dead, white or black. What's more, I don't believe that he ever had either a wife or a sister; and unless he was aided or abetted by a wife or a sister he couldn't have had a brother-in-law, could he?"

"If he chooses to invent a brother-in-law to brag about, why shouldn't he?" I asked. "There's many a man who has written a book to glorify the great deeds of some remote ancestor from whom his own descent was more than doubtful."

"I know that," Harry Brackett responded, as we entered the club and gave our storm-coats to the attendants; "and I know also that there are men so lost to all sense of the proprieties of life that they insist on telling you the latest ignorant and impertinent remarks of their sons of six and their daughters of five. But I hold these to be among the most pestilent of our species — less pestilent only than a man who tells tales about his brother-in-law."

I said nothing in reply to this; but my reserve did not check the flow of Harry Brackett's discourse.

"All the same," he went on, "people have ancestors and they have children, and to boast about these is natural enough, I'm afraid. But a brother-in-law! Why blow about a brother-in-law? Of course it is a novelty—at least I never heard of anybody's working this brother-in-law racket except Cockshaw. And I'll admit that it is a good act, too : with an adroit use of the brother-in-law Cockshaw can magnify himself till he is as great a man as the Emperor of China, who is nephew of the moon, great-grandson of the sun, and second cousin to all the stars of the sky!"

I protested against the vehemence of Harry Brackett's manner, without avail.

"But he's got to be more careful," he continued, "or he'll wear him out; the brother-in law will get used up before the little man gets out half there is in him. No brother-in-law will stand the wear and tear Cockshaw is putting on him. Why, within a fortnight he has told us that his brother-in-law climbed the Jungfrau in 1853, lost a leg in Pickett's charge in 1863, and went down in the *Tecumseh* in 1864. Now I say that a brother-in-law who can do all those things is beyond nature; he is a freak: he ought not to be talked about at this club; he ought to be exhibited at a dime museum."

I tried to explain that it was perhaps possible for a man to have climbed a Swiss mountain, and to have been wounded at Gettysburg, and to have gone down in the *Tecumseh*.

"But if he was colonel of a North Carolina regiment, how came he on board of a

United States iron-clad?" asked my companion.

"Perhaps he had been taken prisoner," I suggested, "and perhaps—"

"Shucks!" interrupted Harry Brackett. "That's altogether too thin. Don't you try to reconcile the little man's conflicting statements. He doesn't. He just lets them conflict."

We had paused in the main hall to have the talk out. When at length we walked on into the grill-room, we found Judge Gillespie, and Rupert de Ruyter, and Cockshaw already getting supper at the round table in the bow-window. De Ruyter called us over, and he and the judge made room for us.

As soon as we were seated, the judge turned to Cockshaw with his customary courtesy, and said, "I fear we interrupted you, Mr. Cockshaw."

"Not at all," the new member answered, with an inoffensive smile. "But as we were speaking of philopenas I was only going to tell of an experience of my brother-in-law. Twenty years ago or so, when he was war-

den of the Church of St. Boniface in Philadelphia, he met a very bright New York
girl at dinner one Saturday night, and they
ate a philopena together—give and take,
you know. The next morning, when he left
his pew to pass the plate after the sermon,
he felt a sudden conviction that that New
York girl was sitting somewhere behind him
on his aisle to say 'Philopena' as she put
a contribution into his plate. He managed
to look back, and sure enough he spied her
in an aisle-seat near the door. So he had
to whisper to a fellow-vestryman and get
him to exchange aisles."

In some tortured manner the talk turned
to churches and to convents. And this led
Judge Gillespie to give us a most interesting account of his visit to the monastery on
Mount Athos, where the life of man is re-
duced to its barrenest elements. When we
had made an end of plying him with questions, which he answered with the courtesy,
the clearness, and the precision which marked his speech as well in private life as on
the bench, the talk again rambled on, rip-
pling into anecdotes of monks and monas-

teries in all parts of the world. Harry Brackett had spent a night with the monks of
St. Bernard in the hospice at the top of
the Simplon Pass; Rupert de Ruyter had
made a visit to the Trappist monastery in
Kentucky; I had been to the old Spanish
mission-stations in Southern California and
New Mexico; only the new member of the
club had no personal experience to proffer.
He listened with unfailing interest as each
of us in turn set forth his views and his adventures, serious or comic. Then when we
had all exhausted the subject, Cockshaw
smiled affably and almost timidly.

"I have lived so quiet a life myself," he
ventured, "that I do not know that I have
ever met a monk face to face, and I know I
have never been inside of a convent; but
when my brother-in-law was a boy, he was
travelling in Brittany with his father, and
one night they were taken in at a convent.
My brother-in-law was given a cell to sleep
in, and over his head there was a tiny cup
containing holy-water; but the boy had
never seen such a thing before, and he
didn't know what it was for, so he emptied

out the water, and put his matches in the little cup, that he might have them handy in the night."

"When was this?" asked Harry Brackett, feeling in his pocket for a pencil.

"In '67 or '68," Cockshaw answered.

Harry Brackett pulled down his left cuff and pencilled a hasty line on it, an operation which the new member of the club failed to notice.

"Oddly enough," he continued, "my brother-in-law saw a good deal of the Breton priests who sheltered him that night, for he was studying medicine in Paris when the war broke out in 1870, and he joined the American ambulance, which happened more than once to succor the brave Bretons who had come up to the defence of the capital. Indeed, he was out in the field, attending to a wounded Breton, at Champigny, when he was killed by a spent shell."

Remembering that Cockshaw had told us before that his brother-in-law was drowned in the *Tecumseh*, I looked up in surprise. As it chanced, I caught the eye of the new member of the club. He returned my gaze in a straightforward fashion, and yet with a certain suggestion of timidity. I confess that I was puzzled. I looked over to Harry Brackett, but he was gazing up at the ceiling, with his pencil still in his fingers.

Then we both turned our attention to the "Gramercy Stew" which the waiter brought us, and which was the specialty of the club. Judge Gillespie and De Ruyter had almost finished their supper when we arrived, and they now made ready to leave us.

"I wish I were as young as you, boys," said the judge, as he rose; "but I'm not, and I can't sit up as late as I used. Besides, I must go to the Brevoort House early to-morrow morning, for I've promised to take Lord Stanyhurst to Grace Church."

"Is Lord Stanyhurst over here?" asked Cockshaw, with interest.

"He arrived this afternoon on the *Siluria*," the judge answered. "Do you know him?"

"I know his son," replied the new member of the club. After a momentary pause he added: "In fact, we are remotely connected by marriage.   He is my brother-in-law's brother-in-law."

Judge Gillespie and Rupert de Ruyter did not hear this, for they had walked away together.

But Harry Brackett heard it, and he sat upright in his chair and cried : "What was that you said ? Would you mind saying it all over again, and saying it slow ?"

"Certainly not," responded Cockshaw, with no suggestion of aggressiveness—with all his wonted placidity. "I said that Lord Stanyhurst's son was my brother-in-law's brother-in-law ; that is to say, he married the sister of the man my sister married.

"Do you know," Harry Brackett remarked, solemnly—"do you know that you have the most remarkable brother-in-law on record ?   A brother-in-law

> so various, that he seem'd to be
> Not one, but all mankind's epitome."

"How so ?" asked the new member of the club, with a stiffening of his voice, as though he were beginning to resent the manner of the man with whom he was talking.

I sat still and said nothing. It was not my place to intervene. Besides, I confess that my curiosity made me quite willing to be present at the discussion, even though my hope of any possible explanation was remote enough.

"I don't want to say anything against any man's brother-in-law," Harry Brackett went on, "but don't you think that the conduct of yours is a little queer?"

"In what way?" asked Cockshaw, with greater reserve.

"Well, in the way of dying, for example," Harry Brackett responded. "Most of us can die only once, but your brother-in-law managed to die twice. First, he was drowned in the *Tecumseh*, and then he was killed at Champigny."

"But that was not—" began the new member of the club, and then he checked himself sharply and said, "Well?"

"Well," repeated Harry Brackett, with possibly a shade less of confidence in his manner, "Well, he was a very remarkable character, that brother-in-law of yours, before he departed this life twice, just as though he had been twins. In fact he died three times, for I'd forgotten his demise in Vienna in 1873, just before the Exhibition opened. His habit of dying on the instalment plan didn't prevent him from putting in his fine work all along the line. I don't suppose that you married the sister of the Wandering Jew or that your sister married the Flying Dutchman, but I confess I can't think of any other explanation. You see I've been keeping tab on my cuff. Your brother-in-law's name is Eli Low, and he is now a partner in Carpenter & Co., the publishers. But he went to California in 1849, and he climbed the Jungfrau in 1853, and he lost a leg at Gettysburg in 1863, and he lost his life by the sinking of the *Tecumseh* in 1864, which did not prevent his being a boy in Brittany a few years later, or his getting killed all over again at Champigny in 1870—although I should think the Prussians would have been ashamed to hit a drowned man, even with a spent shell. And this second demise never interfered with his being president of a lumber company in Chicago at the time of the fire, 1871, or with his going in the

same year to Africa with Stanley to find
Livingstone. But he must have scurried
home pretty promptly, because in 1872 he
was a warden of St. Boniface's in Philadelphia; and then he must have flitted back
across the Atlantic in double-quick time, because in 1873 he was studying with Dr. Spitzer in Vienna, where he died a third time.
So even if he were a cat he would have only
six lives left now. In 1876 he seems to have
gone to Louisville to see the Fourth of July
race between Tenbroeck and Molly Macarthy; and now to-day in 1892 he is a partner
in a publishing house here in New York."

To this long statement of Harry Brackett's Mr. Harrington Cockshaw listened in
absolute silence, making no attempt to inter-
rupt and seeming wholly unabashed. Once
a smile hovered around the corners of his
mouth for a moment only, vanishing as
quickly as it came.

Now he lifted his eyes, and looked Harry
Brackett squarely in the face.

"So you think I have been lying?" he
asked.

"I wouldn't say that," was the answer.

"I'm not setting up codes of veracity for other people. But taking things by and large, I can't help thinking that your brother-in-law has had more than his share of experience. I wonder he doesn't go on the road as a lecturer—or else I wonder that you yourself don't write a novel."

The new member of the club repeated his question : "You think I'm a liar?"

Harry Brackett made no reply.

Cockshaw continued in a perfectly even voice with no tremor in it. "You think that when I told you all these things that you have amused yourself in setting down on your cuff in chronological order, I was telling you what was not so? Then what will you say, when I assure you that every statement of mine is strictly accurate?"

"If you assure me," Harry Brackett answered, "that your brother-in-law died once in 1864, and again in 1870, and a third time in 1873, all I can say is that he wanted to be in at the death, that's all. He was fonder of dying than any man I ever heard of."

"Mr. Brackett," said the little man, "when I told you all these things, one at a time, about my brother-in-law, I never meant to suggest, and I never supposed you would believe, that they all referred to one and the same brother-in-law. They don't. My wife has six brothers, and I have five sisters, all married now—so I have still eight brothers-in-law surviving."

Harry Brackett rang the little bell on the table, and when the waiter came he said, "Take Mr. Cockshaw's order."

(1892.)

ETELKA TALMEYR

ETELKA TALMEYR:

A TALE OF THREE CITIES

I.—LONDON.

THERE had been a full week of fair weather at the beginning of June, and Piccadilly was swept its whole length by the afternoon tide of cabs and carts and carriages, which swirled about the stolid statue of the Iron Duke and eddied away to Belgravia, to Ken· sington, and to Mayfair. The sandwich men who wearily followed each other in single file along the gutter, bearing on their breasts and backs boards announcing " The Messiah " at the Albert Hall, were often splashed by the brisk hansoms emblazoned with the arms of their noble owners. It was nearly four o'clock, and the flood was still rising.

Among those who were borne along by its current were two New Yorkers.

" I used to think," said one of them, Mr. Robert White, " that the chief difference between New York and London could be summed up in a sentence: in America we have clear skies and dirty streets, while in England they have dirty skies and clean streets. But such a week as we have had now spoils my epigram, and gives the British both clean streets and clear skies."

" In dry weather all signs fail," gravely quoted his companion, Dr. Cheever.

" Then I had always been told that the English climate had none of the staggering uncertainty Old Probabilities gives to American climate, and that the British Clerk of the Weather could be counted on absolutely, so that you might be sure as to what was going to happen — if it rained, you might declare it was going to clear up in an hour or so, and when it was fair, you knew that it would pour sooner or later. But after the past ten days, I begin to believe that the British abuse their own climate just as they do our spelling."

"If you will examine the attire of some of the young ladies who are passing us," said Dr. Cheever, "I think you will see that the natives have not maligned their weather. They have been taught by experience to go prepared for any fate."

White laughed gently. "I have noticed," he rejoined, "that the regular June costume of a London girl is a white muslin dress with a pink sash and a fur cape, and then, when she puts on her galoches and takes her umbrella, rain or shine makes no difference to her."

The doctor smiled, but did not respond further.

"I suppose we shall see lots of girls at this concert," White went on. "Is it going to be a very swagger function, as they say over here?"

"Probably," Dr. Cheever answered. "Lady Stanyhurst is very popular with young people, I'm told. But this is really a children's concert we are going to now. Her son is a violinist; he's only fifteen, but he takes lessons of Sarasate. And I heard the Dowager Duchess of Dover say that 'really, you know, his playing isn't half-bad,' and that is their highest formula of praise."

By this time the two friends had arrived before a spacious house facing the pleasant freshness of the Green Park. From the door of this mansion· a carpet had been rolled across the sidewalk; and every minute or two carriages drew up, and their occupants — mostly ladies, and many of them elderly and elaborately upholstered—passed along the carpet into the house.

" Here we are," said Dr. Cheever.

" She has a sizable house, this Lady Stanyhurst of yours," White responded, as they made ready to enter.

They were late, since the concert had been announced for three o'clock; and as they passed up the crowded stairs they heard the metallic notes of two pianos, vigorously pounded by a pair of tall, thin girls, twin daughters of Sir Kensington Gower, K.C.B.

The duet ceased as the two Americans managed to reach the hostess, standing just within the doorway of the drawing-room.

"So glad you were able to come," said
Lady Stanyhurst to Dr. Cheever. She was
a pleasant-faced plump little body. "And
this is your friend? So sorry you did not
hear that charming duet! Those girls of
Sir Kensington's are astonishing — really
astonishing."

White was about to murmur inarticulate
regrets for his tardiness when the hostess
turned from him to greet a later arrival.
He heard Lady Stanyhurst say, "So glad
you were able to come," to a portly clergy-
man; and then the pressure of the crowd
carried him and Dr. Cheever towards the
end of the room, and they found freedom
only when they were in the embrasure of
an open window, whence they could look
across the park and see the clock-tower of
Westminster through the summer haze.
From this coign of vantage they could
survey — if they turned their backs on the
view out-doors — the large rectangular
drawing-room, with the other rooms opening
beyond.

They had scarcely taken up their position when a violin-stand was placed in the

centre of a little open space near the two
pianos in the adjoining room, and a smug-
faced boy of fifteen came forward with a
violin in his hand.   He wore an Eton
jacket, and he seemed very uncomfortable
and awkward.   There was a lull in the
chatter which filled the house, for this was
the son of the hostess ; and the lad began
the "Sarabande" of Corelli.   He did not
play badly for a boy, but the musicians
present must have wondered at the maternal pride which could force the lad to such
a discovery of his inexperience.

When the perfunctory applause had died
away, after the encore which the poor boy
had prepared for, White said to Dr. Cheever,
"And who is here ?"

"All sorts of people," responded his
friend.   "There's the Prime-minister in
that corner talking to the Dowager Duchess of Dover.   There's the editor of the
Epoch, with his wife and five daughters, just
coming in.   There is Dr. Pennington, the
rector of St. Boniface's, of Philadelphia —"

"Are there Americans here besides us ?"
asked White.

"Lots of them," the doctor replied; "and all sorts too. The rector of St. Boniface's there is alongside Dexter, the Chicago wheat operator."

"How did he get here?" White wanted to know.

"Oh, there are worse here than Cable J. Dexter," Cheever returned. "When an American adventurer comes to London with lots of money, it's always a question whether he will be taken up by the police or by Society."

While the two Americans were thus generalizing hastily about London society, the violin-stand had been removed by a footman in white livery, who now returned and raised the top of one of the grand-pianos. Among the little group of intimates of the house who were gathered close to the instrument there was to be noticed a movement as of expectancy. In a minute a young girl came forward and took her seat at the piano.

For a moment she sat silent and motionless, and then, without any suggestion of hesitancy or timidity, she raised her hands and began to play.

As the first bars of Chopin's B. Minor
Scherzo fell upon his ears, Dr. Cheever
checked his friend's gossip with a gesture,
and said, "Why, they've got a musician!"

He and White turned to see the player.
They saw a slip of a girl of perhaps fifteen
or sixteen, her thin face crowned by a thick
mass of black hair, and lighted by a pair of
flaming eyes. As she played on, a spot of
color began to glow on her tawny cheeks.

"That bag of bones has the sacred fire,
hasn't she?" cried White. "See how her
long face is almost transfigured by the
music."

"I wonder who she is," Dr. Cheever
said.

"She's not English, for one thing," returned White. "Neither that swarthy skin
of hers nor that musical temperament is
native to the British Isles."

"Not English, of a certainty," the doctor
declared; "gypsy, possibly, or Jewish —
they are both musical peoples. But she
may be a Slav or a Czech; you can't tell.
The face is expressive, but it keeps its se-
crets, for all that."

"It's the face of a born musician—that's obvious enough," said White, as the power of the performance seized them both. "I wish she hadn't that trick of twitching her eyebrows."

"She has very obvious gifts," the doctor added, "and she has trained herself rigorously. There is will in that jaw of hers, the determination to succeed."

"What will she be in the future?" White queried. "A great artist? A great lady? A great beauty even? Or will she degenerate, and not develop at all?"

"She may be a beauty if she chooses," his friend answered. "She has the raw material of beauty in those strange features of hers. And she is clever enough to be a beauty if she thinks it worth while. It's the exceeding cleverness in the face that impresses one most. Yes, she is devilishly clever that girl; quite clever enough to be a great artist, a great lady, a great beauty — all three — if the chance come. And in the mean while she is interesting to listen to and interesting to look at."

"I wonder," said White, gazing at the

girl intently, " where she came from almost
as much as I wonder where she will go.
What is the heredity that breeds faces and
figures like hers ?   And what environment
will best develop an ardent soul like that ?
Will the future take her up or carry her
down ?"

" Who can tell now ?" the doctor responded. " Look at her mouth—that is
sensual ; and there is cunning in those thin
lips.   With that mouth I should say a girl
might go to the devil—or might hold a
candle to him, if she thought the game
worth it."

" That is to say," White returned, " with
a face such as hers anything is possible in
the future.   In the mean time, I'd like to
know to whom the face belongs now.   It
will have to be an outlandish name to fit
that exotic personality."

When the music ceased and the girl rose
from the piano, Dr. Cheever saw standing
near to him a spare and angular old lady
with a queer little cap askew on her head
under a queer little bonnet.

" Here is the Dowager Duchess of

Dover," he whispered to White. " I'll ask her. She knows everything and everybody, and everything about everybody."

Stepping forward, he said, "Good-afternoon, Duchess."

The elderly lady looked up and recognized the American, and acknowledged his presence by protruding two bony fingers of her right hand, saying, " It's Dr. Cheever, isn't it ?"

" At your service," he replied, " and he wants to ask a favor of you—or at least some information. Who is that girl who has been playing ?"

" Plays very well, doesn't she ?" returned the Duchess. " You could tell at once that she wasn't a lady by her touch—quite professional. And they say she has a voice too—something quite wonderful."

" Who is she ?" the doctor repeated.

" She's a foreigner, of couse—a Pole or a Hungarian, or something of that kind, you know," the Duchess answered. " Her name's Etelka Talmeyr—odd name, isn't it ? But then foreigners are so peculiar. She's the daughter of a music-teacher at

Madame Mohr's, a doubtful sort of character, who ran away and abandoned the child. I believe that she's dead now, and Madame Mohr has kept the girl out of charity. So kind of her, wasn't it? But then she is charity itself. Of course Talmeyr teaches the little girls and makes herself useful about the school. She could do no less, could she?"

Having thus satisfied Dr. Cheever's curiosity, the Dowager Duchess of Dover dropped him an acidulated smile and passed on.

"Kindly old aristocrat, that Duchess of yours," said White, as Dr. Cheever returned to his side. "Every woman her own freezer. Duchess of Wenham Lake, I'd call her."

"I wouldn't call her if I were you," the doctor rejoined, "for she wouldn't come. And you need not abuse her, either, for she told us what we want to know about the thin girl with the fiery eyes."

"Etelka Talmeyr is just the name for her, isn't it?" asked White. "Etelka is Hungarian, isn't it?"

"And Talmeyr is German, I suppose," said Dr. Cheever.

"Well," White added, after a moment's pause, "we know who she is and what her name is. But we don't know what she will be in five years."

"What she will be in five years," the doctor responded, "nobody knows, least of all the girl herself. And yet a face like that has force behind it, and I should not wonder if the woman of five years from now made some of the dreams of the girl of to-day come true."

By this time a duet had begun between a plump girl of thirteen playing the 'cello and her brother, a lad of fourteen, seated at the piano. The rooms were getting more and more crowded as betarded guests continued to arrive.

Dr. Cheever found an acquaintance who had in his hand one of the satin programmes which set forth the order of exercises, and borrowing this for a second, he saw that Miss Etelka Talmeyr was not to perform again. He told his friend.

"Shall we go, then?" asked White. "I

believe that a little turn in Bond Street before dinner might drive my wife's headache
away."

So the two New Yorkers shook hands
with the hostess, and passed down the
thronged stairs and out into the sunshine
of Piccadilly.

II.—NEW YORK.

One evening in February, more than six
years later, Mr. Robert White sat in a corner
of the huge dining-room of the College Club
in New York, eating a lonely dinner. His
wife had gone down to Florida with her
father to avoid the thawing and the freezing
which are commonly characteristic of a New
York February ; she had been away two
weeks, and White was beginning to feel
abandoned. It was Washington's Birthday,
and a holiday often operates to make a
solitary man desperately lonely. The deso-
lation of the occasion was further intensified
by the weather. For two days there had
been a steady drizzle of fine rain, enough to

"MR. ROBERT WHITE SAT IN A CORNER, EATING A LONELY DINNER"

moisten and embrown the heaps of snow in
the streets, but not vigorous enough to wash
these away.   Now a damp mist was rising
from the sidewalks, and a flicker of rain
trickled through it at intervals.   The damp-
ness made it unwise to open the windows of
the dining-room, and the atmosphere was
close and discomforting.

Holiday as it was, White had gone duly
to the office of the *Gotham Gazette*, and he
had written his usual editorial article, putting into it perhaps an undue causticity, due
only to his dissatisfied loneliness; it was an
essay on the gratitude of our republic, as
proved by its keeping the birthday of its
founder, now nearly a hundred years after
his death.   An essay on this theme does
not lend itself necessarily to sarcasm and
irony.

His day's work done, on a day when other
men were doing nothing, White had come to
the College Club in the hope of a stimulat-
ing game of piquet and a dinner with some
congenial friend.   But the club had been
almost deserted, and among the few men
there he had seen none of his intimates.

He was too kindly to abuse the waiter for
the fault he found with the dinner, but he
called for the complaint book and wrote a
sharp protest against the acridity of his
coffee.   Having thus relieved his feelings
somewhat, he walked down to the billiard-
room.

As he entered the room he was met by a
cry of welcome.

" Hello, White ! I say, boys, let's make
White go with us too ! ' When the wife is
away, the husband can play;' there's a
motto for you."

The speaker was a clean-shaven, clean-
looking young fellow, Kissam Ketteltas by
name; and he was just back from three
years of hard labor at a German university.
As he spoke he was coming towards the
door with half a dozen other young fellows.

" Mr. White has the best of it," said one
of them; "this is the kind of day when I
wish I was married.   If I had a wife now, I
could pass the time quarrelling with her."

"To be bored is the proper punishment
of idleness," returned Ketteltas; "and you
haven't done any work since you graduated.

Besides, matrimony is a poor remedy for monotony. 'Anything for a quiet wife;' that's another motto for you !"

"White is a grass-widower now, anyway," said one of the group, an undersized little man with a thin wisp of sandy mustache, "and he had best make hay while the sun shines. So he hasn't any excuse for not coming with us."

This last speaker was little Mat Hitchcock, whom White disliked. He lighted his cigar before responding.

"If you will kindly intermit this coruscation of epigram," he said, "and tell me where it is you want me to go with you, I shall be in a condition to give you an earlier answer."

"We are going to the Alcazar," Ketteltas replied.

"The Alcazar?" White repeated, doubtfully.

"If you had read your own paper last Tuesday," returned the other, "you would have seen that the Alcazar is a new music-hall—something like the London Alhambra, you know; and the Great Albertus is to

make his first appearance to-night—in honor
of Washington's Birthday, I suppose, and
to commemorate the ancient alliance of
France and America."

"Are you all going?" asked White, looking over the group, and remarking in it none
of his own intimates, and even one man he
disliked.

"We've got a big box, and we are all
going," Ketteltas responded; and we want
you to come with us to matronize us. We
will blow you off. So 'don't look a gift
cigar in the mouth;' there's another motto
for you."

"I don't know about going," White began,
hesitatingly.

"I do," the other interrupted. "And I
know you are going. We need you to ex-
pound the ulterior significance of some of
the more abstruse of the Frenchman's songs.
Besides, little Mat Hitchcock here is so
near-sighted that he can't see a joke unless
he has his eye-glasses on, and he has broken
them, and we shall rely on you to explain all
the doubtful allusions to him."

So saying, Kissam Ketteltas seized Robert

White's arm and led him away, only half resisting.

"I suppose this thing we are to see is what
is called a variety show?" White asked, as
the party plunged into the muggy murkiness
of the night.

"It is *called* a variety show, I admit,"
Ketteltas answered, "just as a lawyer's
document is called a brief—and with about
as much reason. But then, if it is always
the same, it is always amusing, for it makes
absolutely no demand on the intelligence."

A sudden flurry of rain forced them all to
button their collars tightly and made conversation difficult. A dank steam rose from
the roadway, and the electric lights gleamed
dully through the mist and the drizzle.

"This is a soggy night, if you like one,"
said Ketteltas, as they came to the vulgarly
decorated entrance of the Alcazar.

"But I don't like one," White responded,
following his guide down a long dark cor-
ridor. "And I don't like to think myself a
fool, either—although I feel like one for
coming to this hole."

"Here's our box," the other said, as the

attendant opened a door. "You won't regret coming; this place has a color of its
own quite worth while seeing. I've been
to variety shows in all parts of the world,
and they are all alike—and all unlike too.
They are great places for studying human
nature. There's a lot of character about a
music-hall—although some of the frequenters
have lost theirs."

The box they emerged into was one of a
series into which the narrow galleries running along the walls were divided by low
board partitions. It was the one nearest to
the stage, and it was perhaps the largest, for
it contained eight chairs, in two rows, with
a long table between them. The hall was
also long and narrow. The floor was covered with more little tables, surrounded by
chairs. There was a small stage at the end,
with a violently painted set of scenery, supposed to represent an Oriental garden. The
decoration of the hall was equally mean and
vulgar. The strongest impression the place
produced was one of tawdry squalor. Men
with their hats on sat at the little tables,
drinking and smoking, countrymen and boys

mostly. Women with obviously artificial complexions were drinking with the men, or moving restlessly up and down the side aisles. The atmosphere was heavy with stale smoke. Robert White wondered why he had come.

When White, Ketteltas, Hitchcock, and the others entered, half a dozen musicians were blaring forth the refrain of a comic song, and the scant stage was filled by the exuberant presence of Miss Queenie Dougherty, the Irish Empress — such the programme declared her to be. It was nearly nine o'clock, and the performance had begun an hour before. Miss Queenie Dougherty was even then singing for the fourth time, in response to three successive recalls. The song she was then engaged on White recognized from having heard it whistled in the streets. It described the prowess of a Hibernian gentleman of pugnacious proclivities, who was besought in the chorus to demolish his antagonist:

> " Hit him one or two !
> Hould him till you do !
> Bate him black an' blue !
>   For the honor of ould Ireland !"

When the Irish Empress had sung this
song to the bitter end, and had at last been
allowed to withdraw, a screen, painted crude-
ly to imitate a glaring Japanese fan, closed
in and hid the stage.

"What's next?" asked little Mat Hitchcock.

"I've a programme," Ketteltas answered.
"Next we are to behold The Staggs, the
Royal Star Acrobats.   That will give me
time for my celebrated imitation of a man
taking a drink.   What will you have, boys?"

Before the attendant had taken their orders the screen on the stage was withdrawn,
and The Staggs came forward in single file.
There were five of them, the foremost a
thick-set, middle-aged man, and the last a
slight lad.   They were all in evening dress,
with black knee-breeches and black silk
stockings and white ties and crush hats.
They bowed to the audience, removed their
hats, and built themselves suddenly into a
human pyramid, with the oldest man as the
base.   Then they removed their dress-coats,
and in their shirt sleeves they proceeded to
perform the customary feats of ground and

lofty tumbling, with a certainty and a neat-
ness which delighted White's heart.   At
length they withdrew, and the screen again
shut off the stage.

"What's next?" asked little Mat Hitchcock again, with the impatience which
was one of his most irritating characteristics.

Ketteltas referred to his programme.
"La Bella Etelka and Signor Navarino in
their great musical and terpsichorean fantasy," he read.   "I remember La Bella
Etelka," he said.   "I saw her in Budapest
two years ago — but she hadn't any Signor
Navarino with her then.   She was a good
looker, rather, but when she danced she
tousled herself all up till she was as fearful
as a Comanche banshee."

When the screen parted again, it was
seen that a piano had been placed on the
stage.   Then an ignoble little man, in a
caricature of a dress suit, led on a tall, dark
woman of striking appearance. He escorted
her to the piano, at which she took her seat;
he prepared her music for her with exagger-
ated courtesy, and when she began to play,

he danced a few eccentric steps behind her back.

As La Bella Etelka took her seat at the piano she faced Robert White, and was scarcely fifteen feet from him. He looked at her without interest, and then suddenly he began to ask himself where he had seen that face before. By the time she had played a dozen bars of Chopin's Waltz in A Minor he had recognized her by the peculiar twitch of the eyebrows. The movement of the wrist was the same also, the carriage of the head, the eyes, even the face — everything but the expression. He did not hesitate more than a minute, and after that he had no longer a doubt that he had seen La Bella Etelka once before—six years before, in London, at Lady Stanyhurst's children's concert, one afternoon in June. La Bella Etelka was Etelka Talmeyr; of that there could be no question, although she had altered strangely for the worse. The foreign look, Slav or Czech, Jewish or gypsy, was unmistakable still; and there was no difficulty in recognizing the high cheek-bones, the fiery eyes, the thick black hair.

But what a pitiful metamorphosis it was
that the bright, youthful girl of six years
ago should be changed already into this
full-blown, vulgar-looking woman.   The expression had been energetic and self-reliant ;
it was now crafty, common ; and the hint
of sensuality in the girl's face was obvious
animality in the woman's.   All the features
had hardened ; all the promise had gone
out of them, all the gentleness, and all the
hope.

While Robert White was thus moralizing,
La Bella Etelka and Signor Navarino were
earning their salary.   She had played the
dreamy and poetic measures of Chopin
with a mastery of the instrument and an
appreciation of the music almost out of
place in that tobacco-smoked hall.   Then,
without warning, she changed the time to
that of the ordinary waltz, instantly vulgar-
izing the music and accentuating the rhythm
as her associate danced more and more gro-
tesquely.   After a while he skipped over to
her, and still keeping time with his feet, he
began playing also.   Almost as soon as he
took his position at the piano she left the

instrument, dancing away with easy grace, and managing her long black train with consummate skill. She waltzed about the small stage decorously enough at first, and then, without warning, still keeping perfect time, she flashed out her foot and kicked her partner's hat off his head. Playing with one hand only, he turned sideways and protested in vigorous pantomime. She danced away from him, sweeping her long skirts; and then she danced back, kicking high over his head as he sat at the piano. The band then took up the tune softly, and Signor Navarino left the piano and skipped towards La Bella Etelka, who tripped lightly up the stage and took his hand, whereupon they came down to the footlights together, each in turn swinging a foot over the other's head, to the roaring applause of the spectators.

It was with growing repugnance that Robert White watched this vulgar exhibition, but he could not take his eyes from the woman's face. As he looked at the low couple pirouetting about the tawdry stage, he recalled every word of his conver-

"THEY CAME DOWN TO THE FOOTLIGHTS TOGETHER"

sation with Dr. Cheever at Lady Stanyhurst's that afternoon in June, six years before. He remembered their speculation as
to the future of Etelka Talmeyr — whether
she would degenerate or develop. She had
degenerated — there was no doubt of that.
Despite the diabolical cleverness Dr. Cheever saw in her face, and the abundant
strength of will he declared her to have, the
girl had not become a great artist, a great
beauty, a great lady. She had become what
White saw before him—a sorry spectacle.
If six years had wrought all this change,
what adventures, what experiences, what
harsh disappointments, and what bitter
griefs must have been crowded into them
to have made possible this obvious moral
disintegration. The woman looked twice
six years older than the girl he had seen six
years before—but then the face was rouged
and plastered and blackened out of likeness
to itself. Besides, as the French say, years
of campaign count double ; and he almost
shuddered to think what hideous campaigns
hers must have been to account for so sad-
dening a transformation.

Another roar of applause awakened White to the fact that La Bella Etelka and Signor Navarino had made their final bow, and were retiring hand in hand.

"They'll get their encore," said Kissam Ketteltas; "she needn't beg for it with those electric-light eyes of hers. She's got more spice in her now than she had in Budapest two years ago."

As La Bella Etelka and Signor Navarino reappeared, Robert White was so saddened by the painful comparison he could not help making between the Etelka Talmeyr of London and La Bella Etelka of New York that he felt a sense of shame in being any longer a witness of the woman's degradation.

He rose, and after a few hasty words of apology to Ketteltas he left the music-hall and went home.

"White's not going to be here to explain the Gallic jests of the Great Albertus to you, Mat," said Ketteltas; "but I'll do my best to replace him."

"Bob White's getting very high-toned lately," little Mat Hitchcock responded;

" he thinks a good deal too much of himself."

" There are lots of us who do that,"
Ketteltas returned ; " ' it's a poor mule that
won't work both ways '—if you want another
motto."

III.—PARIS.

About that time Robert White's father-
in-law, Sam Sargent, the chief owner of the
Transcontinental Telegraph Company and a
striking figure in Wall Street, was planning
a sale of certain of his stocks to an English
syndicate ; and when, some three months
later, Sir William Waring, the head of the
great London banking - house of Waring,
Waring & Company, arrived in New York
on a brief tour of inspection and inquiry, Mr. Sargent seized the opportunity
and gave the visiting financier a dinner at
Claremont. It was a most elaborate entertainment, and the British guest was equally
impressed by the beauty of the Riverside
Drive, then in the first freshness of its

spring greenery high above the noble Hudson, which swelled along grandly below, and by the accumulated wealth of the assembled company. One of the newspapers, in its paragraph on the banquet, the Sunday after, declared that the twenty guests represented more than One Hundred Millions of Dollars.

If this surmise were accurate, then the wealth was not distributed equally among the guests, for there were at least two poor men at the table. Robert White was generally invited to his father-in-law's formal dinners, and on the present occasion he found himself by the side of his old friend, Dr. Cheever.

" Is there any germ theory of wealth ?" he asked the doctor, as they took their seats. "Can you isolate the bacteria, and breed riches at will ?"

Dr. Cheever laughed lightly, and returned, "If wealth were contagious, would you expose yourself to the danger of catching it, or would you come to me to be inoculated against the infection ?"

" I wonder," the journalist answered —

"I wonder whether I should really like to be enormously rich. I doubt if I should care to give up my mind, such as it is, wholly to the guarding of wealth. That must be the most monstrous and enervating of pursuits. Of course it has its compensations. If I were as rich as the rest of our fellow-diners, I'd have my private physician — at least I'd offer the appointment to my friend Dr. Cheever."

"I'm afraid one master would be more exacting than many," the doctor responded. "There is safety in numbers. I took a rich patient over to the south of France last February, and the experience was not so pleasant that I care to repeat it. By-the-way, while I was in Paris I wished you were with me once—"

"Only once?" White interrupted. "Then I'm sure I shall not confer on you my appointment of physician in attendance."

"Once in particular I wished for you," Dr. Cheever replied. "It was because I could have shown you the answer to a question that we had puzzled over together. Do you remember my taking you to a children's con-

cert at the Stanyhursts' one afternoon in
June six or seven years ago?"

"Of course I recall that concert," White
answered, "and I've got something to tell
you about that queer little girl we saw that
afternoon—Etelka Talmeyr."

The doctor finished his soup, and said:
"It was about that same queer little girl
that I was going to tell you something. I
have seen her again."

"So have I," interposed White.

"Have you?" Dr. Cheever asked, in surprise. "I didn't know you had been to Europe since that summer."

"I haven't," White returned. "I saw the
Etelka here."

"Here?" echoed the doctor. "I didn't
know she had ever been to this country."

"She is here now," White said.

"Impossible," cried Dr. Cheever. "If the
prince were in America, I should have heard
of his arrival."

"The prince?" repeated White, amazed.

"Yes," the doctor explained, "She is
now a princess, the little Etelka Talmeyr we
saw in London years ago."

"A princess, is she?" White returned.
"Then the prince must be a queer speci-
men."

"Prince Castellamare is one of the most
charming men in Italy," the doctor explained, "and one of the most dignified."

"Then I should think his dignity would
be shocked at the way his wife exhibits herself here," White replied.

"But she can't be in this country," Dr.
Cheever declared. "She was in Paris when
I left there, the last week in February."

"But I saw her here in New York the last
week in February," asserted the journalist.

"You saw the Princess Castellamare here
last February?" the physician asked.

"I don't know any Princess Castellamare," White responded. "I know only
that I saw Etelka Talmeyr here in New
York in February last. Oh, I can recall the
very date; it was on Washington's Birthday."

Dr. Cheever laid down his fork, and looked
at his friend in astonishment. "Why, it was
on Washington's Birthday that I saw her in
Paris," he said. "I can fix the date easily,

because it was at a reception at the American minister's that I saw her—a reception given in honor of the national holiday. How could the Princess Castellamare be in two places at once?"

"Barring she was a bird," quoted the journalist, "and she is almost light enough on her feet to be one. But, joking apart, you begin to puzzle me. I don't know anything about any Princess Castellamare, but I do know that I saw La Bella Etelka here in New York on the evening of February 22d, and I am sure that La Bella Etelka and the Etelka Talmeyr we saw in London that June afternoon are one and the same person."

"This is really very extraordinary," said the physician. "For my part, I know nothing of any Bella Etelka, whoever she may be, but I know for a fact that on the evening of February 22d I went to a reception at the American minister's in Paris, and there I saw the Princess Castellamare, and I heard her sing; and, beyond all question, she is the Etelka Talmeyr we heard play that afternoon in London."

"See here, doctor," White remarked, earnestly, "the Etelka Talmeyr we saw in London can't have been twins, can she? She can't have doubled up and developed into a princess in Paris and into a variety-show performer here in New York. It is too early along in the dinner for us to see double in that fashion; so we had best tell each his own story in his own fashion, and then we can compare them, and so discover which of us has been befooled. You can begin."

"My story is simplicity itself," the doctor said. "On the evening of Washington's Birthday I went to a reception at the American minister's in Paris. There was music, of course; we had a contralto from the Opéra, a tenor from the Opéra Comique, and two or three of the best amateurs of the American colony. Just before the supper was served I was at the door of the music-room, when I heard the first notes of Schumann's 'Warum' sung by a mezzo-soprano, a voice of wonderful richness and softness and flexibility, trained to perfection. Besides her method, the vocalist had a full understanding of the dramatic character of the music. I pressed forward, and I saw before me, standing beside the piano, a very handsome young woman, tall, stately, with raven hair, with a splendid throat, with flaming black eyes, and with the same curious trick of twitching her eyebrows we had remarked when we heard that little bag of bones play in London. The likeness was obvious—indeed, it was unmistakable. The face had softened; the lines had filled out; the contour was flowing now, and not sharp; the complexion was more delicate, but there was the same spot of color in the cheeks, and there was the same resolute glance from the eyes. Where there had been determination to succeed, I could now see the determination which had succeeded. I asked who she was, and I was told that she was the Princess Castellamare. The prince's first wife was an American; she died four or five years ago, and he was inconsolable till he met his present wife. They were married last summer. She had been a Mademoiselle Talmeyr, and she had made her first appearance at La Scala in Milan the year before. I remembered that the Duch-

ess of Dover had told us that Etelka Talmeyr had a voice. What more natural than
that she should tire of teaching and go on
the stage? As I looked at her across the
room, I recalled our talk about her, and I
saw that she had developed into a great
beauty, a great artist, and a great lady. I
gazed across the room, and although her
face was rounded now, I could still detect
the firmness of the jaw which had made
such a development possible."

"Is that all?" asked White, as his friend
paused.

"That is all," the doctor answered. "I
have told you how I came to identify the
Princess Castellamare with the little Etelka
Talmeyr of years ago. I confess I am curious to hear your story, and to discover how
you can possibly think that you have seen
her in this country when I left her in Europe."

"My story is quite as short as yours, and
quite as plain and quite as convincing,"
White declared; and then he told the doctor how he had been alone on the evening
of Washington's Birthday, how he had dined

at the College Club, how Kissam Ketteltas
had taken him to the Alcazar, how he had
seen La Bella Etelka and Signor Navarino
in their great musical and terpsichorean
fantasy, how he had recognized La Bella
Etelka as the Etelka Talmeyr he and the
doctor had seen in London years before,
how he also had noticed the characteristic
twitch of the eyebrows, how he had been
saddened that the girl had not developed,
but had degraded and vulgarized. " But,"
he concluded, " that La Bella Etelka, whom
I saw at the Alcazar on the evening of February 22d, is Etelka Talmeyr I am absolutely certain."

" And I am equally certain," the doctor
declared, " that the Princess Castellamare,
whom I saw at the American minister's in
Paris on the evening of February 22d, is
Etelka Talmeyr."

" Well," said Robert White, as he began
on his Roman punch, " we cannot both of
us be right."

" Either you are wrong," the doctor asserted, " or—"

" Or you are," White interrupted. " On

the 22d of February Etelka Talmeyr was either in New York or in Paris; she could not have been in both places. I say she was in New York, and you say she was in Paris. There is no possibility of reconciling our respective statements, is there?"

"None whatever," Dr. Cheever answered. "But I will allow you to withdraw yours if you like."

"I'll do better," returned the journalist. "I will prove it; at least I will prove that I am right in thinking that Etelka Talmeyr and La Bella Etelka are one and the same person."

"I'd like to see you do that!" said the physician, sarcastically.

"You mean that you wouldn't like to see me do it," White retorted. "But see it you shall, and with your own eyes. According to your own story, your Princess Castellamare is now in Europe somewhere."

"She was in Paris when I left there," said the doctor, "but she has very likely gone back to Rome now with her husband."

"Exactly so," White went on. "Your

Princess Castellamare is at least three thousand miles off, and you can't show her to me. But La Bella Etelka is still here in New York at the Alcazar, and I can show her to you. And I propose to do it, too. You shall be convinced by your own eyes. Dine with me to-morrow, and we will go to the Alcazar together, and you shall see for yourself."

"I will dine with you with pleasure," the doctor replied. "And I will see for myself."

"For the present," White declared, "let us have peace. Let us possess our souls in patience. Let us do justice to my father-in-law's hospitality. It is now the middle of May, and the game-laws are in force, so I draw your attention to the Alaskan ptarmigan which is now about to be served."

"I didn't know there were any ptarmigan in Alaska," said the doctor, innocently.

"There isn't," White responded, as he helped himself to the prairie-chicken.

IV.—NEW YORK.

The next evening Dr. Cheever and Mr. White sat side by side in the Alcazar, the tawdry gilding of which was already beginning to be tarnished by tobacco smoke. They arrived in time to see Miss Queenie Dougherty, the Irish Empress, respond to her third encore, and to hear her sing about "The Belle of the old Eighth Ward," the chorus of which declared that

> "When Thady O'Grady
> Came courtin' Nell Brady
> There wasn't a lady
> As pretty, as witty, in the whole of the city."

They had the pleasure of seeing the Human Sea-serpent give his marvellous exhibition of contortionism in a Crystal Casket of real water. Then Prince Sionara, the Royal and Unrivalled Japanese Juggler, made butterflies out of bits of paper, and forced them to flutter hither and thither about the stage, after which he spun a top in the air and caught it on the edge of a sword, and did other strange feats, as is the custom of Japanese princes in variety shows, concluding with his Celebrated Cyclone Slide on the Silver Wire from the upper gallery backward to the stage.

"Now," said White, as the Japanese bowed himself off the stage — "now we are to have Etelka Talmeyr," and he handed his programme to Dr. Cheever, pointing to the lines announcing La Bella Etelka and Signor Navarino in their great musical and terpsichorean fantasy.

The screen which served as a drop-curtain parted in the middle, and disclosed the piano on one side of the stage; and then the wretched little parody of a man led on his tall, dark, striking partner, and escorted her to the instrument.

"Don't you see the likeness?" cried White. "It is unmistakable."

"Of course I see it," the doctor answered. "But it is a likeness only, a likeness such as one may see any day."

As La Bella Etelka seated herself at the piano and struck the opening notes of

Chopin's Waltz in A Minor she looked out across the footlights at the audience, and her eyebrows twitched automatically, as they had done when White had watched her before.

"Did you see that twitch of the eyebrows?" he asked, triumphantly. "Did you ever see any one who had that trick and who looked like that except the Etelka Talmeyr we saw in London years ago?"

"Yes," the doctor answered, "I have seen the Princess Castellamare; she looks like this poor creature here, and she has that same twitch. And, as I told you last night, I am sure that she is the Etelka Talmeyr we saw in London."

"You are unconvinced still?" White asked.

"Quite unconvinced," Dr. Cheever responded. The Princess Castellamare was a Mademoiselle Talmeyr, and she is now about the age the Etelka Talmeyr we saw ought to be by this time. This Bella Etelka of yours is five or ten years too old."

"She looks older than Etelka Talmeyr might look, I'll admit," the journalist returned; "but she has had a hard life, obviously, and she shows it. A woman doesn't keep her youth in an atmosphere like this."

"That is true enough," the doctor acknowledged.

"Let's put two and two together," White went on. "It is seven years since we were in London, and Etelka Talmeyr was then fifteen or sixteen, so she may be twenty-three now. La Bella Etelka here looks twenty-six, or thereabouts; but will you declare that she is really more than twenty-three?"

The doctor gazed intently at La Bella Etelka as she and the little Italian gyrated about the stage.

"No," he said, at last. "This woman may be any age you please, and she is astoundingly like the girl we saw in London. I see the resemblance more and more the longer I look at her. She has the sensual mouth I noticed then, and the cunning lips too. . In fact, I see in this woman here the development of all the less pleasing characteristics of the Etelka Talmeyr we speculated about seven years ago, just as I saw

in the Princess Castellamare the development of all her pleasanter qualities. In the
little girl in London there were the possibilities of a beauty, an artist, a lady, and the
Princess Castellamare is all three. But
there was in her also the possibility of a
degradation such as we see on the stage
now."

"In other words," commented White,
" you think that the little Etelka Talmeyr is
a female Jekyll and Hyde, with the added
faculty of sending the bad Hyde on this
side of the Atlantic, while the good Jekyll
on the other marries a fairy prince ? That's
a picturesque explanation of our dilemma,
of course, but isn't it a little lacking in
scientific probability ?"

Dr. Cheever did not answer for a minute.
His eyes were following the tall figure in
the long silk dress as it floated languidly
across the stage in time to the music of the
waltz. He extracted a coin from his pocket,
dropped it in a slot on the back of the chair
next to him, and released an opera - glass ;
with this he took another long look at the
dancer.

Then handing the glass to White, he said, "This woman is much older than she looks. There are signs which are unmistakable. Look at the wrinkles around her eyes and below her chin. She is at least ten years older than the Etelka Talmeyr we saw in London."

White took the glass and gazed in his turn. "You are right," he admitted, frankly, "she does look older; but, for all that, I think—" Here he broke off suddenly and called to a man who was about to take a seat near them. "Brackett!"

"Hello, White," responded the gentleman thus hailed, turning suddenly and dropping into the nearest chair. "I didn't know you took in this sort of thing often."

"I don't," White answered. "I come as little as possible; and to-night we are here for a purpose, Dr. Cheever and I. Dr. Cheever, Mr. Harry Brackett."

The two men bowed. Harry Brackett offered the doctor his box of cigarettes.

"I am here regularly. They'll let you smoke here, and then you see all sorts of things."

"I called Brackett over," said White to the doctor, but so that the new-comer could hear him, "because I believe he can help us out. He has been a reporter, and he has managed a panorama, and last winter he wrote an alleged farce - comedy for Daisy Fostelle, and he probably knows more people and more different kinds of people than any other man in New York."

"That's true," assented Harry Brackett. "You never can tell when knowing a man will come in handy."

"Do you happen to know the manager of this place, or the stage - manager?" asked White.

"I know them both," was the response. "I know the manager best, but Zeke Kilburn has a swelled head since he got this show. He owns the earth, and has a first mortgage on the rest of the solar system. But I guess I can work him. What do you want?"

"We want to find out about La Bella Etelka here, and whether she used to be called Etelka Talmeyr, and whether she is any relation to the Princess Castellamare."

15

" I guess she's no relation to any princess, or we should have seen it in the paragraphs before this," said the ex-manager of the panorama. " I don't know anything about her, but I believe that she is married to that little chap who does a dancing act with her. She is very jealous of him, too ; flared up like a volcano the other night because he complimented Queenie Dougherty on her new song. There came near being a hair-pulling scrap ; but Zeke Kilburn happened along just then, and he separated them. Tell me just what it is that you want to know, and I'll see what I can do for you."

Thereupon White set forth with perfect fairness the point at issue between the doctor and himself, and explained why it was they were interested in knowing whether the Etelka Talmeyr of London was the Mademoiselle Talmeyr of Milan, now the Princess Castellamare of Rome, or whether she was La Bella Etelka of New York.

" I think I see what you want," Harry Brackett declared, as he rose to his feet. " And I guess I can get it for you.   Keep my seat for me, and I'll come back as soon as I can."

Lighting another cigarette, and throwing the empty box under the chair, Mr. Harry Brackett left them, and walked away to the manager's office.

On the stage La Bella Etelka and Signor Navarino were concluding their musical and terpsichorean fantasy; side by side they advanced from the scenery at the back to the trembling footlights, each in turn lifting a foot over the other's head as they danced down, to the wild applause of the spectators.

White and Cheever waited patiently as the successive numbers of the variety entertainment followed one another. The Senyah Sisters, two pretty girls, with lithe and graceful figures, climbed to a double trapeze in the arch of the proscenium, and went through the usual intricate performance commingled of skill and danger. Then Mr. Mike McCarthy gave his World-renowned Impersonation of the Old-time Darky, in the course of which he sang an interminable topical song, accompanying himself on the banjo. Finally came the last number on

the programme, a so - called burlesque ex-
travaganza, compounded of noisy songs and
halting verses.   Bored as they were and
weary, White and Cheever felt sorry for the
poor actors, straining themselves vainly to
give a double meaning to words devoid of
any.

At last, when the tether of their patience
was stretched almost to the breaking-point,
Harry Brackett reappeared, and dropped
into the seat they had kept for him.

"Did you discover anything?" asked Dr.
Cheever.

"Is La Bella Etelka the Etelka Talmeyr
we saw together in London," White inquired,
"or isn't she?"

"One at a time, please," Brackett responded.   "And give me a cigarette, if
you've got one.   Then I'll tell you what
I've found out."

Robert White proffered his cigarette-case.

Harry Brackett helped himself. "Thanks,"
he said.   "Egyptian, ain't they?   Too rich
for my blood nowadays; I stick to the native article."

Dr. Cheever handed him a lighted match.

"Thank you," he went on, puffing at his cigarette. "Well, I found out several things. I've got the key to your mystery. And the answer isn't at all what either of you thinks."

"How so?" began White; "isn't—"

"Best let him tell his story in his own way," the doctor interrupted.

"That's what I think," assented Harry Brackett. "And I'll be as brief as I can, too. I happened on Zeke Kilburn at the door here, and I got him to take me behind. First thing we stumbled on the little Dago — Signor Navarino. Zeke knocked him down to me, and I froze to him at once, and took him into the cork-room and blew him off to a bottle, and got him to talk about himself. In less than five minutes I turned him inside out as easy as an old kid glove. There isn't anything he wouldn't tell me if I asked him. So I dropped a question or two about La Bella Etelka. And she wasn't in London seven years ago."

Dr. Cheever looked at White with an air of triumph.

"For the good and sufficient reason,"

Harry Brackett continued, " that she was then in South America, singing in comic opera—' La Perichole,' you know, and the 'Timbale d'Argent.' She had been in London once upon a time, about ten years ago, when she was a music-teacher, or something of that sort—"

" So she was once a music-teacher in London ?" White interrupted. " Then I don't see why—" Then he checked himself.

Harry Brackett continued : " She was a widow, and she got stuck on a Dutchman, who came over with a French comic opera company, and she just dropped everything and went off with him. Four or five years ago he died — that's the Dutchman — and she drifted into the variety business. She met the little Dago in Budapest a year or two ago ; he's a mean little cuss, but she has married him all the same. She's worth a dozen of him easy. From things he let on, I sized her up, and I made a guess as to her relation to the Princess Castellamare."

" I see," said White. " The princess is her younger sister."

" Then you can't see straight," Harry

Brackett retorted, "because the princess isn't her sister. I made a guess, as I say, and I wanted to find out if I'd struck it. So I shook the little Dago, and I went back on the stage and found Kilburn again, and I got him to introduce me to La Bella Etelka, who was just ready to go on in the burlesque. She is a good-looking woman, for all she's forty."

"Forty?" cried White. "Come, now, that's impossible."

"It's true," Brackett returned. "She confessed to it—indirectly, but it's straight enough. I complimented her, and I made myself as solid as I could. You see I had my idea, and I wanted to find out about it. So at last I made a brace. I said, suddenly, 'There's a friend of mine in front, just back from Paris, and he tells me he saw the Princess Castellamare just before he left.' She flushed up, and asked, 'How was she? Is she well? I wish I could see her.' Then I told her what the doctor here had said— how the princess was looking beautiful, and how she sang like an angel. Then she turned on me all of a sudden, and said, 'How did you know about my daughter?'"

"Her daughter?" White interrupted.

"Yes," Brackett answered; "that was my guess. And it rang the bell the very first shot too. She grabbed me by the arm and said, 'She doesn't know about me, does she? The prince doesn't suspect?' And then I knew I'd sized the thing up about right."

"I confess I do not quite see—" began the doctor.

"It's simple enough," explained Harry Brackett. "She'd run away from London and abandoned her daughter, leaving her in good hands, though. She had kept track of her always, and she was delighted when she heard of the success of Mademoiselle Talmeyr at Milan. Then she was just going to write to her daughter, a little doubtful of the reception she would get, or how the daughter would take the news that the mother was alive she had so long thought dead, when all at once she heard that Mademoiselle Talmeyr was going to marry Prince Castellamare. Then she knew she had better not say a word. She had heard enough about Italian princes to suppose that they wouldn't like a mother·in·law on the variety stage doing a song-and-dance act. So long as the daughter thought the mother was dead, the old woman reckoned that she had better stay dead. And I left her just paralyzed with wonder that I had dropped on a secret she didn't suppose anybody else in the world knew. And it is funny, isn't it?"

" The maternal instinct seems to have awakened very tardily," the doctor remarked.

" It was pretty slow, for a fact," Brackett admitted. " But I guess it was there all the same—slow but sure."

" Well," said White, "if she keeps away from her daughter she will enjoy the very highest feminine felicity—the luxury of self-sacrifice."

" Yes," Brackett smilingly agreed. " I think that she was about as glad that I knew about it as she was sorry."

At that moment the music of the brazen orchestra swelled out, and part of the scenery at the back of the stage fell apart, disclosing the Fairy Queen glittering in the glare of the calcium-light, and with her opulent figure daringly revealed by her splendid costume.

"I wonder," remarked Robert White, foreseeing the end of the play, and rising with his two friends—"I wonder what your Princess Castellamare is doing in Rome now, while La Bella Etelka is on exhibition here in New York?"

"That's easy enough," Harry Brackett answered, as they turned their backs to the stage and walked towards the door. "There is five or six hours' difference in time, isn't there? Well, it's nearly twelve o'clock here, so I guess your princess over there is getting her beauty-sleep—that is, unless she sits up five hours later than her mother, which isn't likely."

(1892.)

THE END.

THE ODD NUMBER SERIES.

16mo, Cloth, Ornamental.

DAME CARE. By HERMANN SUDERMANN. Translated by BERTHA OVERBECK. $1 00.

TALES OF TWO COUNTRIES. By ALEXANDER KIELLAND. Translated by WILLIAM ARCHER. $1 00.

TEN TALES BY FRANÇOIS COPPÉE. Translated by WALTER LEARNED. 50 Illustrations. $1 25.

MODERN GHOSTS. Selected and Translated. $1 00.

THE HOUSE BY THE MEDLAR-TREE. By GIOVANNI VERGA. Translated from the Italian by MARY A. CRAIG. $1 00.

PASTELS IN PROSE. Translated by STUART MERRILL. 150 Illustrations. $1 25.

MARÍA: A South American Romance. By JORGE ISAACS. Translated by ROLLO OGDEN. $1 00.

THE ODD NUMBER. Thirteen Tales by GUY DE MAUPASSANT. The Translation by JONATHAN STURGES. $1 00.

Other volumes to follow.

Published by HARPER & BROTHERS, N. Y.

☞ *Any of the above works will be sent by mail, postage prepaid, to any part of the United States, Canada, or Mexico, on receipt of the price.*